ACE

A   BASEBALL   STORY

By L. P. Vine

Dedication

Dedicated to the fond memory of my parents, Max and Jo, my brother Dave and my son Nicholas.

I'd also like to thank my wife Kelly, who has been by my side for 35 years; my daughter Lauren and her family, Dan and Jackson. My son Luke, who helped inspire the writing of Ace along with my son Nicholas. My granddaughter Mia, who has been like a daughter to me, and Matthew Connelly.

Besides family, I can't forget Mr. William Wall, now a retired English teacher, for all his guidance over the years in terms of my writing.

To Helena Wasilewski, for being my friend and technical supervisor on this project.

To Rebecca Wasilewski, for additional editing.

To CreateSpace for allowing self-publishing available to everyone.

And let us not forget all the volunteers and parents who participate in all aspects of team sports. Without them, most sporting events would be non-existent.

Table of Contents

The Interview Begins

"Welcome to the Sports News Network's weekly series "Baseball Today." I am Skip Freeman and today's show will feature a candid interview with World Series pitcher Tim "The Ace" Sherman. As you may already know, Ace's team, the Portland Lumberjacks had the worst record in the major league in 2018. This year with the help of Ace Sherman, the Lumberjacks became one of the few teams to go from last to first place and win the World Series. Not to mention Ace's no-hitter in game seven.

Our three-hour special presentation will begin with highlights from Ace's regular season games to the playoffs, to the World Series, and finally our exclusive interview with Ace himself. Let's go over to our New York studio with Janet Steed where you'll view some of the greatest game highlights of this young rookie's career."

"And cut!" The show's director shouted as Skip Freeman's TV smile relaxed with a deep sigh.

"Is Ace in the studio yet?" Skip asked with concern. "I haven't much time to get this interview taped."

"He arrived about five minutes ago," the director confirmed. "He'll be in studio seven in ten minutes. The camera crew is ready and waiting."

In studio seven sat the twenty-one-year-old Ace with a makeup person dabbing powder on his cheeks and forehead. He seemed tired, almost annoyed, and not in any mood to conduct another interview.

"Ace, how are you feeling today?" Skip asked with his arm outstretched to handshake.

"Tired," Ace said shaking hands. "Too many jet plane trips this week, I can't wait to go to my hometown in Pennsylvania and get some rest."

"I can't say that I blame you," Skip replied. "You've become the talk of the town just about everywhere in the United States. Are you ready to begin our interview?"

"I'm as ready as I'll ever be," Ace sighed. "But I don't know what else I could possibly talk about. I mean, how many interviews does the public need to know about my no-hitter in game seven of the World Series?"

"Are you guys ready to begin taping?" The director asked.

"You bet," Skip returned.

"Ten seconds," the director warned. "And roll 'em."

"Welcome back to Baseball Today. I am Skip Freeman and beside me sits Tim "The Ace" Sherman for an exclusive interview seen only on SNN. I'd like to take a different approach in today's interview and go back long before you became a national hero," Skip informed him. "Are there any stories you can think of that might interest our younger viewers in the audience? You know, stories from the Amateur Baseball Youth League, otherwise known as the ABYL, and how your early career began?"

"You know something, Skip?" Ace admitted. "I think I just might have that story you're looking for. It's about the time I briefly quit baseball at age twelve and about the coach that made me look at the game of baseball in a whole different way."

"That's funny you should mention your old coach," Skip said with a wide grin. "Would his name happen to be Cecil Blake?"

"How did you know that?" Ace asked surprised.

"Hey, this is SNN," Skip bragged. "We're no small time

news network. As a matter of fact, he's in the studio right now. Would you care to see him?"

"Would I?" Ace's eyes widened. "I haven't seen him since I was drafted into the major's. Where is he? Can I see him now?"

"Turn around," Skip smiled. "He's standing right behind you."

Ace turned his head and his eyes began to tear. He rose from his seat nearly knocking his chair over to embrace his old coach.

"Coach Blake!" Ace wept. "It's so great to see you."

"Easy, Ace," Coach Blake grimaced. "You're crushing me. I'm not as young as I used to be."

The two longtime friends separated and Ace wiped away a tear and gave a quick sniffle of his nose.

"Did you get the World Series tickets I sent you?" Ace wondered. "I was looking for you in the stands."

"Oh, I was there and thank you," Coach Blake informed him. "But you know me. I can't sit still for too long at a game. I was never one to be in the stands."

"Oh, I know that well," Ace laughed. "I think after each ABYL game, the maintenance crew had to bring in a wheel barrel full of dirt to fill in the trench you made from pacing back and forth."

"I don't think I was that bad," Coach Blake smiled. "But you kids sure did give me a few grey hairs."

"Excuse me, but," Skip interrupted. "Now that you fellows have been reacquainted, let's get back to our topic of Ace's career in the ABYL. Where would you like to begin, Ace?"

"Well to be honest with you, Skip," Ace told him. "My career with Coach Blake only spanned a brief period in that league. Only six games to be exact. Six of the best games I can remember."

"C'mon," Skip said in disbelief. "How can any game be better than your no-hitter in game seven of the World Series?"

Coach Blake and Ace turned to each other and smiled. "I think there was one game that might have been slightly more exciting than that," Coach Blake chuckled. "Wouldn't you agree, Ace?"

Ace's cheeks turned a shade of red as a smile beamed across

9

his face when he said, "Oh, yeah. One game in particular," Ace nodded. "I'll never forget that one."

"Well this best be good," Skip sat confused but eager to listen. "Let's take a quick commercial break and when we return, you can fill in our audience on this so-called exciting game. We'll be right back."

Coach Blake vs. Coach Newport

"Welcome back to SNN's weekly series "Baseball Today." I'm Skip Freeman, and on today's show, we've reunited Tim "The Ace" Sherman and his ABYL coach Mr. Cecil Blake. Between the two of them, they seem to know of a game more exciting in Ace's career than the no-hitter Ace threw in game seven of the 2019 World Series. So Ace, do you want to tell us about this great game?"

"I think the only person who can really begin this story is Coach Blake. The game was just a mere formality compared to what took place prior to the game."

"Then I guess it's up to you, Coach Blake," Skip interrupted. "Care to begin?"

"Gladly," Coach Blake opened. "Like Ace was saying, I was a newcomer in Spindale, Pennsylvania, only residing there for six months. I worked at the Newport Sneaker plant as head of production control. One day at work I saw a notice on the bulletin board. It stated that the ABYL was in need of coaches. I had coached a team when I lived in California, and I chose to sign up.

My team was dubbed with the sponsor's name of "Mary's Dress Barn" and was the living joke of the league. Not only did the kids have the weight of being called a bunch of Mary's, but as we approached mid-season, we were zero wins and six losses. To make matters worse, in game seven we faced the unbeaten team in the league called the "Newport Sneaks."

We were looking for our first win. The Newport Sneaks were striving not only for Pennsylvania's ABYL's win streak record, but the country's. They hadn't lost a game in the past three seasons and were on their way to another perfect season. That is, of course, unless Mary's Dress Barn could beat them.

After the third inning, surprisingly, we were only behind by one run. The league only allows a pitcher to throw three full innings per game, so I saved my best pitcher to close the game."

"So this is where Ace came into play," Skip interrupted. "Let me guess. Ace strikes out the next nine batters, and during the game you somehow take the lead, ending the Newport Sneaks' win streak.

12

To me, that doesn't seem more exciting than the no-hitter in game seven of the World Series."

"I wish I had Ace at the time, but he played for the Newport Sneaks. He was their closing pitcher for the last three seasons. Ace was the reason this team was undefeated for so many games. No one could hit his high-powered fast ball. This win streak was more his than anybody's."

"Now I'm really starting to get confused," Skip admitted. "I thought you coached Ace?"

"I did," Coach Blake insisted. "But not yet."

"So why are we talking about this game?" Skip wondered. "I thought we were talking about your so-called exciting game."

"Maybe I can explain," Ace said with eyebrows raised. "As Coach Blake said, my team the Newport Sneaks, were up by one run. My coach at the time was Coach Newport. He was the owner of the Newport Sneaker factory and Coach Blake's real life boss. Coach Newport didn't want to take a chance on losing this game so to insure us of a win, he wanted me to do something that's been kept secret to this day."

In the dugout, Coach Newport took me aside and said, "Wait for my signal." He tugged on his left ear with his right hand then slowly dragged his finger across his throat. "You know what this means, don't you?"

"Not again," I pleaded. "Not another bean pitch."

"You want to win, don't you?" Coach Newport asked with shoulders raised. "Then wait for my signal. I'll let you know who's going to go down."

I hated the bean pitch. I didn't want to hurt anybody, but I would do what Coach Newport asked. I believed in my coach because our team's win streak showed me that he knew what he was doing.

When the first batter took the plate, I realized he was a friend from school. I had hoped he wasn't the one to be beaned. With one eye, I glanced at the batter and with the other, I glimpsed at Coach Newport. No signal was given, and I hurled a curve ball out of the strike zone. The ball had blown by him as he took a strike with a late swing. I eventually struck him out along with the next batter when the opposing pitcher walked up to home plate.

I loved to strike out pitchers because they were like me, trying not to let anyone get on base without a fight. I completely forgot about Coach Newport's signal and didn't even look his way. I was going to have some fun.

"Strike!" the umpire shouted after I tossed my hardest fastball. The batter seemed impressed and stared back as we exchanged smirks.

"Time out!" Coach Newport yelled and drew everyone's attention.

His face showed anger and his index finger seemed like a magnet, drawing me toward him.

"What's wrong Coach?" I asked, standing before him along the first base line.

"Are you asleep out there?" He yelled but with a whisper. "Didn't you see my signal?"

"But he's the pitcher," I begged. "Let me strike him out."

"Who's calling the shots here? Are you the coach here or am I? You'll sit the bench the rest of the season if you don't do what I say."

"I'm sorry Coach," I said trembling with my head down. "I'll look for your signal. I promise."

"All right then," Coach Newport grinned. "Make sure you aim for his hands."

"But, but…" I stuttered.

"Go!" He yelled.

I stood back on the pitcher's mound and thought how difficult my next pitch would be. His hands were behind his head.

"Play ball!" the umpire shouted as the batter took his stance. I glanced over at Coach Newport, and the signal was given. He tugged on his left ear with his right hand then slowly dragged his finger across his throat.

I took a deep breath, followed through with my windup and

hurled the ball. I had so much power behind that pitch that the batter had little time to react. He ducked his head out of the ball's way, leaving his hands exposed. The ball landed squarely on his thumb of his pitching hand, then ricocheted off and grazed him in the nose.

"Oh my gosh!" I could hear the crowd and I rushed to the plate to see the damage I had caused. Coach Blake immediately ran out from his dugout while his player lay across home plate crying and spastically kicking his feet.

"Take it easy, Pete," Coach Blake tried to comfort him. "You'll be all right. Somebody get me an ice pack!"

Panic had struck the playing field as the boy's hysterical mother ran over to her son.

"I knew he'd get hurt someday," she cried. "I just knew it!"

I felt a hand on my shoulder that startled me. It was Coach Newport's hand.

"Get back on the mound where you belong Ace," he said giving me a wink. "You don't need to see this."

At that point, I was no longer having fun. I had just purposely hurt someone and for what reason? I knew I could've struck him out. I stood on the mound squeezing a new ball as hard as I could. If I had enough strength, I would have crushed it.

A round of applause filled the crowd as the injured player left the field. His mother's arm was draped across his shoulder and I could still hear him sobbing as a pinch-runner took his place on first base.

"Play ball!" the umpire shouted, and I reluctantly glanced over at Coach Newport. No signal was given, and a new angry batter swung away, missing my next three pitches.

As our team entered the dugout, Coach Newport greeted me with a wink and a firm pat on my back.

"Good job, Ace," he said with a grin. "You're up at bat."

This was the last place I wanted to be. I was sure I'd be the target of some other pitcher's revenge. I stood in the on-deck circle taking a few swings as the opposing pitcher warmed up his arm. I concentrated on his speed so I could ready myself to duck if he tried to bean me.

"Coming down," the catcher warned the second baseman.

"Balls in!" the umpire yelled to the players warming up in the outfield.

I strolled up to the plate looking for a fire in the pitcher's eye. One of revenge. As I raised my bat, I could see that none was present. He seemed nervous. I don't think this player ever pitched before and was more concerned about getting the ball in the strike zone than he was about braining me.

"Time out!" Coach Newport yelled to the umpire. "Time out!" he cried on his way to home plate.

"Time out for what?" The umpire replied. "Let's get on with the game."

"I'd be happy to but . . . aren't they supposed to have nine players on the field?" Coach Newport rose up his hands. "There's only eight."

The umpire glanced about the field, and his head bobbed to

the count of eight players. By then Coach Blake took the field in a fury.

"Well, we would have had nine players if your pitcher didn't nearly kill one!" Coach Blake shouted. "We'll still beat you with eight."

"But league rules state that you need at least nine players to compete or it's a forfeit," Coach Newport pointed out.

"C'mon," Coach Blake said in disbelief. "We can't forfeit the game now! The game is so close."

"Mister Blake," Coach Newport said raising up his nose. "Rules are made up for a reason. I think we should let the umpire decide."

"But they're just kids," Coach Blake defended. "I'm sure half of these kids missed supper just to be here and play. Let the kids play ball."

Coach Newport ignored his plea and arrogantly turned to the umpire and asked, "Is it a forfeit or are you going to take it upon yourself to change league rules?"

The umpire had no choice in the matter. Reluctantly he said, "It's a forfeit," as he slowly removed his face mask. "Game goes to the Newport Sneaks."

Questions like, "What's going on? What happened?" filled the crowd as the players left the field. Coach Blake removed his hat and slapped it across his leg on his way to his team's dugout.

"It's a forfeit guys," he told his baffled team. "Line up and shake hands. We lost again. I'm sorry guys."

After the game, the ride home with my parents turned into a fight.

"How did you let that pitch get away from you like that Tim?" My mother asked with concern. "That's the third kid you've hit in the last two weeks. I hope he's going to be all right."

"It's called intimidation, Jane. Right, Tim?" My father insisted. "It's all part of the game. All the pros use that tactic," he continued as he drove. "First you toss one by his chin to back him off the plate. Then you aim for the outside corner and with any luck, the batters backed off far enough to miss the pitch. It's like a chess game. It just so happened that the pitch got away from Tim and he beaned the kid. Hey, look at it this way," my father bragged. "Tim's only twelve years old. He's got all of high school and college to fine tune his arm. With his arm, the pro scouts will be hearing about him. They'll be watching him throughout his career."

"Well, I think Tim should call the boy he hit and apologize," my mother insisted.

"Apologize!" My father raised his voice. "Apologize for what? It's not like he did it on purpose. It's all part of the game. I mean, if you plan on playing sports with the notion that you're not going to get hurt, then you shouldn't be on the field in the first place. Everyone has the option of taking the easy ride as a fan to sit in the stands or watch it on TV."

"Well, if not apologize," my mother sympathized. "It would be a nice gesture to call and make sure he's all right."

"That's the trouble with women about sports," my father

theorized. "You just don't understand the game. Like I said before, it was just an accident. No apologies necessary. End of subject."

"If nobody's going to call," my mother confirmed. "I will. You men are all alike when it comes to sports. It's win, win, win, no matter what the cost."

My father said nothing in return and gripped the steering wheel as he stepped on the gas. I sat silently in the back seat knowing it was no accident as an eerie silence overran the car.

Ace became expressionless in his studio chair with a withdrawn look on his face. He showed signs of regret thinking about his past and Skip Freeman took notice.

"I guess you've felt the pressure of the game of baseball at an early age," Skip kept the interview moving. "I mean, what's a twelve-year-old to do? Listen to the coach and play or disobey and sit on the bench? Then, the aftermath. A young boy gets hurt. Parents arguing. The guilt of beaning someone on purpose. It takes real character to deal with all that stress at age twelve."

"It sure does," Coach Blake added. "But the events that

23

unfolded after that game, I'm sure will really grab your interest."

"Well, I think it's time for a station break," Skip informed them. "Then we'll return with SNN's candid interview with Tim "The Ace" Sherman and special guest, Coach Cecil Blake, Tim's former ABYL coach."

Skip Freeman's smiling face faded as the camera switched to a commercial.

A Conspiracy Unfolds

"We're back," Skip greeted his TV audience. "And we were talking about Tim "The Ace" Sherman's early career in the ABYL. My next question would be to you, Coach Blake. During the last segment of the show, there was no mention of you ever coaching him or about this exciting game that you and Ace talked about earlier. To be honest, I'm confused. At which point in Ace's career, did you actually start coaching him?"

"Let me put it this way, Skip," Coach Blake smirked. "If you're ever in Spindale, Pennsylvania, and you ask anybody about Ace and me, you'll either get a cold shoulder or the quickest directions out of town. Ace and I became the center of controversy in the ABYL."

"Controversy! What kind of controversy?" Skip asked with skepticism. "This is the ABYL we're talking about, not the pros."

"In Spindale, the ABYL is like the pros," Coach Blake

pointed out. "I realize that time on this show is limited but I'll try to explain if you'll permit me."

"We've got plenty of time for any stories of interest about Ace Sherman," Skip confessed. "I'm sure most of our TV audience will agree. Please continue." Coach Blake leaned back in his chair and continued the story.

My wife and team manager, Betty, had phoned the parents of Pete, the boy who was beaned in the last game. It turned out that he had fractured his thumb due to Ace's fastball and would be lost for the season. Mary's Dress Barn now faced the possibility of forfeiting the remainder of the season. Not only was I in need of a ninth player, I needed another pitcher. As head coach, I had to react promptly.

This was my first year in the Pennsylvania ABYL and I was unfamiliar with the league rule for finding another player at mid-season. Not knowing who to contact, I approached my boss at work who happened to be Coach Newport.

I stood before his secretary in the plush lobby and asked, "Would it be possible to speak with Coach Newport?"

"You mean Mr. Newport," she corrected and smiled.

"Why yes, of course," I blushed.

"And you are?" she returned.

"I'm Cecil Blake from production control. It's kind of important that I see him if he's not too busy. It'll only take a minute of his time."

"Well, he's scheduled for a meeting in twenty minutes," she informed me. "I'm very doubtful that he'll see you at this time. Would you care to make an appointment?"

"Like I said before, it's fairly important," I insisted. "Could you please check?"

"Have a seat Mr. Blake," she said slightly annoyed. "I'll go see if he'll be available."

"Thank you . . . and, oh Miss," I said as she neared the office door. "Please tell him I'm the coach from Saturday's game."

"I'll tell him Mr. Blake. I'll be right back," and she knocked and entered Mr. Newport's door. Moments later she reentered the lobby saying, "He'll see you now, but keep it brief."

"Thank you," I said relieved and hastily entered his massive office. I stood in awe glaring at the shelf of polished trophies of past ABYL championships. Alongside each trophy was a team picture with Mr. Newport included in every photograph.

"Mr. Blake," Mr. Newport opened. "Having problems with production in the shop?"

"As a matter of fact, no," I informed him. "Production couldn't be better."

"Then, why this urgency to see me?" He said straightforward. "I'm a busy man with a busy schedule."

"I know you're busy, but I'm new to the ABYL and need your advice on the dilemma I'm facing."

"Dilemma!" Mr. Newport said with sarcasm. "What kind of dilemma could you possibly have coaching a kids baseball team?"

"As you may recall in Saturday's game, your pitcher beaned one of my players. As it turns out, he'll be lost for the entire season."

"What a shame," Mr. Newport seemed unconcerned. "Is that your dilemma? That seems like an easy problem to fix. Just have another player take over as pitcher. Problems solved. That was easy, wasn't it?"

"Not exactly," I explained. "My dilemma is that I only have eight remaining players and will forfeit the rest of the season if I don't find someone soon. I've already contacted three players who quit the team earlier in the season, but they all refused to rejoin the team. I just don't know what to do."

"I'm not really sure how the league would handle this situation," Mr. Newport scratched his head as he thought. "They might just disband the team and disperse the players amongst the other teams. Maybe that might be the best thing for your kids seeing your win-loss record. Or should I say, your loss record."

"Win or lose, I try to make the game fun for the kids," I defended. "Most of the kids on my team don't even care about winning. They just want a chance to play. It's the only way they'll learn."

"That's the difference between your team and mine. My kids can taste victory before each game starts. They all have a certain fire and determination to give it their all. Our win streak speaks for itself."

"Anyway, I'm still one player short," I said as my temper began to rise. "Do you think I should speak to the league commissioner?"

"I would suggest reading up on the guidelines set in the rule book," Mr. Newport stated. "And if you can't find any information on the subject, then I would consult the commissioner."

"I thought of looking it up in the rule book," I said embarrassed. "But I seemed to have misplaced my book early on in the season. I just about tore my house apart trying to find it."

"Then that would explain your ignorance of the eight player forfeit rule in Saturday's game," Mr. Newport insulted. "And you're in charge of production control for my company? I hope you do a better job with my company's internal affairs than you do with your team."

"I take my job very seriously, Mr. Newport," I defended. "I merely misplaced the rule book. To be honest with you, I didn't think I'd have a need to consult it."

"Preparation is the key to success," Mr. Newport proclaimed. "You've got to know the rules whether it is a business or just a game."

"I couldn't agree with you more," I admitted, not needing to be lectured. "But unfortunately, my rule book is lost."

"My time with you has just about expired. I have a meeting in five minutes. Why don't you contact Bruce Rogers in the accounting department? He's the ABYL commissioner."

"I didn't realize that," I said unaware. "Thank you for your time and help."

"And Mr. Blake," he raised an eyebrow and said, "Make sure you contact Mr. Rogers on your lunch break."

"Oh, I intended to," I nodded, wanting to tell him what I really thought of him. "I'll let you know how I make out."

"That won't be necessary," Mr. Newport said unconcerned. "I'm sure I'll hear about the results one way or another. Good day, Mr. Blake."

Once I was back in my office, I paged Mr. Rogers on the interoffice intercom.

"Hello, Bruce Rogers speaking," he answered somewhat bored.

"Mr. Rogers," I opened. "I'm Cecil Blake from production control and I understand you're the ABYL commissioner."

"That's correct," his voice came alive. "How can I help you?"

"I'm one of the coaches in the league and due to a recent injury to one of my players, I'm down to only eight players. Right now, I stand to forfeit the rest of the season if I can't find another player. I spoke with Mr. Newport on the subject, but he seemed out of touch with how the league handled placing another player on my team."

"You spoke with Mr. Newport and he didn't know?" Mr. Rogers seemed surprised. "That's strange."

"And why is that strange?" I asked out of curiosity.

"It's strange because Mr. Newport and I helped amend most of the rule book. It was unprofessionally written. I'm surprised he couldn't help you."

"He had a meeting to attend and maybe he didn't have time to go over all of the details. I think that's why he referred me to you."

"If I remember correctly, in this situation, as a coach, you are allowed to pick a player from the top ranked team, providing that team has a player to spare."

"Yikes," I cringed. "That would be Mr. Newport's team."

"Unfortunately, yes," he concluded. "I wouldn't want to be in your shoes right now."

"So how does that work?" I asked for a further explanation of the rule. "Do I just pick a name out of a hat or do I pick a player to fill the position I most desperately need?"

"This is where things get complicated," he admitted. "The way the teams are picked is that during tryouts, every player is rated by the coaches. Being a coach, you're familiar with that process?"

"Yes," I confirmed. "The kids are rated from one to ten, one being the best and ten being the worst. Then the names are put into a pool, and some computer program makes up the teams so that each team has at least one player of each rank. That way the teams are somewhat balanced with talent."

"That's correct," he added. "That way, one team won't have ten number one ranked players while another team has ten number ten ranked players. It's a very good program. As a matter of fact, one of our programmers from the computer department wrote it."

"So how do I know which player to pick from Mr. Newport's team?" I wondered.

"It goes like this," he explained. "If the player on your team that most recently became injured was ranked as a number six, for example; you would only be allowed to pick a player of the same ranking, a number six from Coach Newport's team."

"The only problem I have now is that I don't have the ranking lists for my team or Coach Newport's."

"That's not a problem," he assured me. "I'll email both team rosters to your office. I just need to know the name of your team."

"Oh, um. . . Mary's Dress Barn," I said feeling embarrassed.

"Good enough," he concluded. "And good luck. You're going to need it. I don't think Mr. Newport is going to be too happy about losing one of his players. Especially with the win streak he has going for his team. That's all he ever talks about."

"There's really not much I can do about it. I have to do what's best for my team. I'm sure he'll understand seeing how he's so bent on playing by the rules."

"Like I said before, good luck," he gave a snicker and ended his message.

It had been a hectic day at work and before I left my office, I checked my computer for any interoffice email. The computer screen read, "You've got mail." When I opened my email, I saw Rosters as the subject, and sure enough, two attachments were included. I clicked on print and out rolled the two rosters from the printer.

I had a team practice scheduled at 5:30 and I didn't want to be late. I grabbed the rosters and exited the office. On my way to the field, I passed several fast food restaurants but had no time to stop. My stomach let out a long repetitious growl as I entered the field parking lot.

Two bicycles were leaning against the outside wall of the dugout and two players were in the field having a pass. I dropped the bulky equipment bag and stared into the vacant parking lot, anticipating more players. To my dismay, by 6:00, only four kids had showed.

"Okay, guys," I yelled out to the kids. "Why don't you warm up your arms a bit? I think we'll work on pitching tonight seeing how Pete is lost for the season. I'll be in the dugout looking over the roster sheets. Hey, Joey, why don't you get on the catcher's gear and I'll be with you guys in a minute. I hope you're wearing a cup."

In the dugout, the roster sheet was rolling with the wind like tumbleweed. I was lucky to stomp on it with my foot before it blew away. A muddy footprint covered the team name so I scanned the list of names looking for Pete's ranking.

"Let's see," I said under my breath as I read out loud. "Number one-Timothy Sherman-pitcher. Whoops. This is Coach Newport's roster."

I scanned the other roster and came across Pete's ranking at number four. That's when I made an unusual discovery. I noticed that only one of the other players names from this list were on my team. I glanced at the top of this list and in bold print it read, "The Newport Sneaks." I wiped away the mud that hid the other team name, and under the thin, brown smear read, "Mary's Dress Barn" with Tim Sherman at number one. The rest of the names were on my team except for one other, a boy named Jerry Mason.

"Wow," Skip broke into Coach Blake's story. "A little conspiracy going on in small town Spindale, Pennsylvania," Skip's voice heightened with intrigue. "So it turns out that someone had tampered with the rosters. But who? The computer programmer?

37

"Nope," Coach Blake insisted. "I confronted him at work and he said he merely wrote the program and put it on a flash drive. He gave the flash drive to the commissioner and that was the last he ever saw of it."

"So it was Bruce Rogers, the commissioner," Skip concluded. "But why?"

"It wasn't him either, because I think if he had done any tampering, he wouldn't have emailed the original rosters to me."

"This is intriguing," Skip could barely keep his composure. "So who was it?"

"Is there enough time on the show to continue?" Coach Blake asked. "We haven't even spoken of the great game that Ace and I remember so well."

"Well, you can't stop now," Skip paused and looked into the distance. "But I guess you'll have to. It's time for a commercial."

A Scandal Exposed

"Here we are, once again," Skip Freeman announced, "with SNN's exclusive Ace Sherman interview. When we left off, Coach Blake, Ace's former ABYL coach was telling us how, at an early age, someone recognized Ace's talent. This person would stop at nothing to make sure Ace was on his team. Even if it meant tampering with the computerized printouts of the team rosters. Maybe Coach Blake can shed some light on the subject as to why this unknown person would want Ace so badly?"

Coach Blake stared into the camera and continued the story where he had left off earlier...

At first, when I discovered that Ace was originally supposed to be on my team, I thought maybe it was just a typographical error. I didn't want to go falsely accusing someone of tampering with the rosters without any real proof. After all, it was just the ABYL, and no real harm was done. My main concern was that I still needed a ninth player for my team. With a game soon approaching, I had to confront Mr. Newport about getting a player from his team.

Prior to my lunch break during work, I headed to Mr. Newport's office hoping he would be there. His secretary, who was nibbling on a cookie at the time, abruptly swallowed and wiped away any crumbs from her mouth with a napkin.

"I'm sorry," I apologized. "I didn't mean to interrupt your lunch."

"That's quite all right, Mr. Blake," she smiled. "I'm quite used to it. How can I help you?"

"I was wondering if Mr. Newport was in or did he already leave for lunch?"

"He's just about ready to leave," She informed me. "And he won't be back for the rest of the day. Would you like me to ask him if he has time to see you?"

"I would appreciate that if you don't mind."

She stood up from her chair and paused before knocking on his door. She turned to me lightheartedly and said, "And it's fairly important, right?"

"Extremely important," I replied with a smirk. "Please tell him it concerns the baseball league."

She knocked, entered his office and then returned with her shoulders raised, "I'm sorry. He said he's too busy right now."

I stood dumbfounded. I didn't know what to do. I only had three days to get a player from his team or I would forfeit my next game. I had to act fast.

"I don't mean to be a pest," I said uncomfortably. "But could you please tell him that I found a discrepancy in the original team rosters."

"I'll try," she said reluctantly and knocked on his door.

"What is it now," I could hear Mr. Newport yell from behind the door. She fearfully tiptoed into his office. "What?" I overheard him shout. "Send him in!"

She scurried out of his office cringing and said, "He'll see you now," then rushed past me toward the ladies room.

41

"Mr. Blake," he scolded. "You're beginning to get on my nerves over this ABYL dilemma that you insist it on being. Now, what's this discrepancy you found in the rosters?"

"Before I get onto that subject, I just thought I'd let you know what the commissioner told me as to what to do about finding my ninth player."

"Is that what you're wasting my time about?" He said infuriated. "I told you I'd find the outcome of that issue sooner or later!"

"But there is a need for me to speak to you about it," I explained. "It turns out that to get my ninth player for my team, I have to choose that player from the top ranked team. That would be your team, Mr. Newport."

"Oh, I see," Mr. Newport lowered his tone. "I was unaware of that."

"That's why I'm here. I needed to discuss that with you," I told him. "I need that player for an upcoming game."

"Well, that will be simple," he said with confidence. "I'll go over my roster tonight and choose a player for your team. I'll inform that player that he has to report to your team. I think I have too many outfielders anyway."

"I wish it was that simple," I explained. "It turns out that league rules state that the rank of my injured player must be replaced by a same ranking player from your team. Trouble is, when I received copies of both our team rankings, I discovered a misprint on both lists. I found that unusual."

"What kind of a misprint?" Mr. Newport's voice began to rise. "How could that be? It's all computerized."

"I know. That's what I don't understand. It would appear that my injured player, Pete, who was ranked fourth, and another player were supposed to be on your team. Not only that, two players on your team were originally picked for mine."

"And who might those two players from my team be?" he asked clearing his throat.

"I know this will come as quite a shock to you, but one of the players is Tim Sherman. The other boy, I can't recall his name."

"Well, if you think I'm going to hand over Ace, you're crazy," he hollered. "Ace is ranked at number one. There's no way I'll trade a number one-ranked player for a number four!"

"But that's beside the point," I found my own voice climbing. "Ace is supposed to be on my team."

"Well, I'm not going to give him up," he said stubbornly. "How can I take a kid of Ace's caliber off an undefeated team and stick him on a team that's an embarrassment to the league? What's your team's record now, zero and seven?"

"I'm just trying to do what's fair," I reminded. "Wasn't it you that said, 'you've got to know the rules, whether it is a business or just a game.' Well, I'm playing by the rules even though the rule we're discussing doesn't even apply."

"What do you mean the rule doesn't apply? You need a fourth ranked player and that's what you'll get."

"But Ace was originally supposed to be on my team in the

first place. Seeing how I have to pick at least one player from your team, it's pretty obvious that it should be Ace."

"Well, I disagree," he said slamming his fist down on his desk. "I think we're going to have to get the commissioner involved on this one. I'll meet with him today, and he'll notify you on his decision before the day's end."

"Have it your way Mr. Newport," I said with a sneer. "I'll be waiting for a decision."

As I left his office, I could hear him shout, "Kimberly, get Mr. Rogers on the phone and tell him to get his butt in my office, pronto!"

"Yes, Mr. Newport," she said trembling. "Right away, Sir."

Later that day as expected, Mr. Rogers stepped into my office and shut the door behind him.

"We've got a problem," he said rather sullen. "Mr. Newport will not give up Ace."

"What is it with that guy?" I said disappointed. "I explained everything to him about the roster misprint and that Ace is supposed to be on my team. Why can't he just accept it?"

"I know, I know," he sympathized. "But he just doesn't want to hear it. He thinks that just because he signs our paychecks that he owns us."

"And what's that supposed to mean?" I asked, assuming Mr. Newport had gotten his way like a spoiled child.

"What it means is that since I'm commissioner and I'm employed by Mr. Newport, I'm supposed to rule in his favor."

"This is outrageous," I yelled with my arms folded across my chest. "How can you make a decision with such a conflict of interest involved? So I take it that your ruling is with Mr. Newport?"

"I haven't decided yet," he said with his head bowed. "Believe me. I know you're right. I honestly think I can lose my job if I side with you. I can't take a chance to lose my house, my car, and my future over an ABYL decision."

"Do you really believe he would fire you from your job over

this?"

"Yes, I do," his voice lowered to a whisper. "I probably shouldn't be telling you this, and if you repeat what I'm about to tell you to anyone, I'll deny ever saying it. This is more than just about Ace or Mr. Newport's obsession with winning. It goes way beyond that. This is all part of an advertising scheme to increase sales for the Newport cleat line of sportswear. Mr. Newport believes that if his team breaks the country's ABYL win streak record that everyone will want to buy Newport cleats. That's going to be his sales pitch. Did you ever notice that all the coaches either work at the sneaker plant or have outside contracting jobs like mowing the company lawns? If they don't let Mr. Newport win, like me, these people face losing their jobs or contracts with the company."

"You know, in a businessman's point of view, I've got to hand it to Mr. Newport," I said honestly. "It definitely is a well-constructed advertising campaign. The only problem I have with it is that it's dishonest. If Newport's team were to break the record, it would be one of the biggest lies in the sports world. And what about the kids on the losing teams? I mean, some of these kids play their

47

hearts out at game time. It really bothers me to think that he would use kids to make a profit."

"Maybe if you look at it this way," Mr. Rogers appealed. "If they do surpass the country's win streak record, and they will, the ad campaign should pay off. Think of all the new jobs and money it will create for the families of all those kids. It'll be great for the town's slumping economy."

"Is that what this is all about, money?" I said shaking my head. "Do you know one of the main reasons I took on the job of being a coach?"

"Because you like working with kids?" Mr. Rogers asked unsure.

"Yes, that's part of it," I told him. "But the main reason is that nobody gets paid. It's all volunteer work, just for the kids. If it wasn't for these sports leagues, you'd find a lot more kids hanging out on street corners, doing drugs, or becoming couch potatoes with a joystick in their hand. This whole mess really disappoints me."

"I feel bad," Mr. Rogers admitted. "But I need to keep my

job. I've got three kids of my own to feed."

"So then it's final. You're ruling in Mr. Newport's favor?"

"What else can I do?" he refrained.

"Wait a minute." An idea came to mind. "Remember what I said earlier about this being a conflict of interest. Couldn't you possibly get the state commissioner to rule on it?"

"And just how would I explain our situation with him?" He said in sarcasm. "I can picture myself on the phone saying if I don't rule in Mr. Newport's favor I'll get fired from my job. The next thing you know, it'll be on the front page of the newspaper and I'll get fired anyway."

"You don't have to tell the state commissioner the real situation," I explained. "A little white lie won't hurt anybody."

"And what might this white lie be?"

"Oh, let's see," I stopped to think. "I've got it. Tell the state commissioner that you have two brothers that are coaches and briefly explain about the roster misprint and the required trade. Tell

49

him that your conflict of interest is that if you side with one brother and not the other, one of your brothers will be angry with you no matter what you decide."

"You know something," Mr. Rogers agreed. "That just might work. I have his phone number in my office. I'll go give him a call right now and see what he thinks."

"Thanks, Mr. Rogers," I gratefully replied. "But we need a decision today. Hopefully he'll have a fax machine and he can send us his ruling immediately. Please stress the fact that we need a written document of his decision."

"I'll do that, Mr. Blake," he assured me. "I'm glad I came here and spoke to you about this rather than just siding with Mr. Newport."

"So am I," I smiled in return and extended my arm out to shake his hand. "And could you do me one more favor when you get a chance? Could you email me the rest of the team rosters? I'm curious to see how many other kids from Mr. Newport's team should be playing elsewhere."

"After I talk to the state commissioner, I'll send them over to you. By the way, how can I reach you if I learn of a decision after working hours?"

"I'll be at the ball field," I smirked. "It's my turn to groom the infield."

"I should have known that's where you'd be," Mr. Rogers laughed as he left the room.

The sun began to set, darkening the infield as I raked. I could feel the dropping air's temperature as it chilled the sweat on my body. An unfamiliar car entered the parking lot with its headlight flickering on and off to draw my attention. A short beep of a horn caused me to lay down my rake, and I went to see who was in the idling car. It was Mr. Rogers.

"I've got the decision, Cecil," he said holding the document out his car window.

"And," I said abruptly.

"He ruled in your favor," he laughed. "We pulled it off. Ace and that other kid, Jerry Mason, have to be moved to your team. Isn't that great?"

"Yeah, but I don't know if I should make that other kid come over to my team. I only need one player. That's mainly what this is all about."

"Well the paper says that both players must go," Mr. Rogers pointed out. "I think you'll have to abide by that ruling."

"Maybe I'll use the other player as a bargaining chip. I'll tell Mr. Newport he can keep him as a gesture of good sportsmanship."

"Yeah, no sense in getting too many people involved," he agreed. "Like you said, you only need one player to keep from forfeiting the rest of your games. I'll let you two coaches decide on the fate of the other player."

"So what happens if Mr. Newport still won't give me Ace, then what?"

"I took care of that," he grinned. "Read the last paragraph of the letter."

"Just tell me. It's too dark to read anything on this letter."

"Well, the letter states that if the Newport Sneaks' coach does not agree with the state commissioner's ruling, that coach will be suspended for the remainder of the season. I think with that hanging over Mr. Newport's head, he'll hand over Ace without too much fuss."

"That was good thinking on your part," I admitted. "I guess you could say we've covered all the bases."

"I thought it was quite clever of me to have the commissioner add that little clause in the decision. I let him know what a shrewd individual Mr. Newport was."

"Speaking of shrewd individuals, remember today when I asked you to send me the lists of all the team rosters?"

"Yeah, I sent them. What did you find out?"

"I didn't find out anything. When the pages rolled off the printer, all that were printed were the names of each team followed by a blank page. There weren't any players listed. I think a shrewd individual might've erased all the team lineups."

"Gee," Mr. Rogers said with eyebrows raised. "I wonder who that shrewd individual might be."

"I wonder," I returned with a laugh.

"This is incredible," Skip Freeman interrupted. "So it was Mr. Newport, the millionaire businessman that changed, and then completely erased all the team lineups?"

"No, I never said that," Coach Blake insisted. "We never had any real proof that he changed or erased anything. There were so many people involved that it could have been anyone who had access to the company's computer. It really didn't matter at the time. The state commissioner's ruling was final. Ace Sherman was to play for Mary's Dress Barn, but we let that other player remain with the Newport Sneaks. We didn't want to trade one of our players for him."

"So Ace," Skip turned to him. "How did you feel when you discovered that you'd be playing on a team with a record of zero and seven?"

"Angry," Ace returned. "That's when my baseball career almost ended at the age of twelve."

"Well, I'm getting a signal from that annoying director that it's time for another commercial," Skip regretted saying. "When we return, we'll be discussing how Tim "The Ace" Sherman nearly quit baseball entirely. We'll be right back."

The Quitter

"Ace Sherman, a quitter? I find that hard to believe," Skip opened glaring into the camera. "Welcome back to SNN's exclusive interview with Tim "The Ace" Sherman. When we left off, Ace was about to tell us how he nearly quit baseball at the early age of twelve. Ace, would you care to explain?"

The camera panned over to Ace as he drifted back to his childhood.

My father had a distressed frown on his face as he spoke on the phone. At the time, I hadn't known who he was speaking with and was eager for him to end his conversation. My head slowly tracked the motion of his hand as he gently set the receiver down. I couldn't wait to go to practice any longer.

"Okay, let's go," I said with my worn out baseball glove tucked under my arm.

"Tim," my father sighed. "That was Coach Newport."

"Aw, don't tell me he canceled practice again," I presumed. "I wanted to try out my knuckleball pitch. I think I'm starting to get the hang of it. I've been practicing every day with Eddie next door after school. He didn't cancel, did he?"

"I'm afraid I have some bad news for you, Tim," he said staring me right in the eyes. "I don't know how to tell you this, but…" he hesitated to rub the back of his neck with his hand. "That was Coach Newport on the phone, and he said you've been traded to another team."

"Traded!" I said outraged. "No one ever gets traded! But why?"

"Remember that kid you beaned in the last game? Well, it turns out he'll be lost for the season."

"Yeah, so," I interrupted. "What's that got to do with me being traded?"

"I guess that team needs another player or they'll forfeit the rest of the season," he explained.

"But there's plenty of other kids in the league that can go," I began to cry. "Why me?"

"I don't know," my father put his hand on my shoulder. "Mr. Newport tried to explain some silly rule but it didn't make any sense to me. I think that the other coach is being spiteful because you beaned his player. Maybe that's why he chose you. His team hasn't won a game yet, and maybe with you on the team he thinks he can finally win one. Who knows why? You know coaches and their egos."

"But it just isn't fair," I sobbed. "It was an accident," I lied. "I don't want to play with those losers. Those kids stink."

"Coach Newport tried his hardest to keep you on his team. He even told me he brought it up as far as the state commissioner and failed. They decided it was you that had to be traded. I just don't understand how they can expect any kid, not just you, to play on another team at mid-season. How can they overlook the success you've had with this team over the last three and a half seasons? You'd think they'd make an exception to the rule in your case."

"Well I'm not playing for Mary's Dress Barn!" I yelled. "They're the worst team in the league."

"So you're going to quit the league?" My father asked unsure.

"I may as well quit," I complained. "Playing on that team would be like playing on no team at all. This really stinks. I was just getting my knuckleball to the point where I could start using it in a game. It just isn't fair."

"You'll find out later on that many things in life aren't fair," my father consoled me. "But if you quit now, you'll never know if that knuckleball pitch will ever work. Anyway, your new coach will be calling you tonight. If you're going to quit the league, you better let him know so he can find another player. It wouldn't be fair to his team to forfeit their games if you know you won't be playing. I'll leave that decision up to you."

"I'm quitting," I sobbed. "There's no way I can play on that team."

"Maybe you should think about it first," my father advised.

"Right now you're upset and I don't think you're thinking too clearly. To be honest, I'd really hate to see you quit. It's an easy habit to start and a hard habit to stop."

"There's nothing to think about, Dad!" I raised my voice. "My season's over."

"I can't make that decision for you," my dad seemed disappointed. "When Coach Blake calls, be sure to tell him your decision. If you want my opinion, I think you're making a terrible mistake."

I was furious and stormed up to my bedroom. I slammed my door behind me and wrathfully cleared off the trophies atop of my dresser with a violent swoop of my hand. They clattered against each other as they hit the floor with one figure breaking away from its stand. It was last year's 2008 MVP trophy.

A tear rolled down my cheek as I thought about the decision I was about to make. I didn't want to quit baseball, but I didn't want to play for Coach Blake. I hated Coach Blake.

A faint ringing of the phone in the background caught my

attention. I sat huddled on my bed hoping the call wasn't for me. I heard the clock ticking in the silence and then heard my father call my name. I pretended not to hear him and hastily sprawled out on my bed burying my face into my pillow. My father's footsteps echoed through the hallway leading to my room, and I pressed the pillow tightly around my face as if to hide.

"Tim," my father called out as he swung open my door. He paused and let out a sigh. "What on earth happened in here?" He shook his head as he said, "Coach Blake is on the phone. I hope you've made your mind up." He set the cordless phone beside me and left the room.

I peeked from beneath the pillow and saw that I was alone. I stared at the phone not wanting to speak as the ticking of the clock rang in my ears. Hesitantly, I picked up the phone and rudely cleared my throat to let Coach Blake know I was there. I didn't want to open the conversation.

"Hello, Tim," he said unsure. "Is that you?"

"Yes," I sniffled. "Hello, Mr. Blake."

"I believe Coach Newport told you the news of the trade. Do you have any problem with that?"

"I don't know," I said in remorse, not wanting to speak. A brief silence soon followed.

"Would you like a further explanation as to why you were chosen to join our team?" Coach Blake sympathized. "I'm sure you must be wondering why."

"No," I returned coldly. "My father explained it all to me."

"All right then," Coach Blake concluded. "We're going to have a special practice tomorrow at 5:30 at Newport Field. This will give you a chance to meet your new team, although I'm sure you know most of the kids from school. Any questions?"

"Nope," I said unconcerned, wanting to end our conversation.

"Okay," he seemed uncertain. "I'll see you tomorrow. If something should come up and you can't make practice, my phone number is 555-1958. You might want to write that number down."

"I'll remember" I said, not knowing a single digit of his phone number. I don't think I heard a word he said.

"I guess that'll do it. I'll see you on the field. I'll be looking forward to having you on the team." Coach Blake finished.

"Yeah, me too," I said in jest and pressed the off button on the phone. "But don't hold your breath, because I won't be there."

"So, Coach Blake," Skip Freeman interrupted. "I can only assume that Ace never showed up for practice. How did you handle that situation?"

"At first, I thought that maybe the Shermans had other plans for Ace that he was unaware of. After all, practice was being called on very short notice. I did make the best of it, though, because I still had to break the news to the team that Ace would be replacing Pete. I sat the players in the dugout and explained the status of the team's future.

"Okay, guys, time for a team meeting," I told the players as they sat fidgeting on the bench awaiting my announcement. "In case some of you don't know by now, Pete fractured his thumb in the last game and will be out for the season."

"So who's gonna pitch? Not me, I hope," Ted, the second baseman said.

"No, not you, Ted," I pointed out. "Not any of you for that matter."

"You mean I'm not gonna pitch anymore?" Mike, our other pitcher blurted out. "Someone's gotta pitch."

"You'll still be pitching three innings a game Mike," I explained. "But with the loss of Pete, we're in need of one more player to keep us from forfeiting the rest of the season. That's why I gathered you guys for this special practice. We've got a new player joining our team, and although he once played against us and beat us, he's on our team now. I want all you guys to treat him like he's been on our team since day one."

"So where is he?" Nick the first baseman asked. "And who is he?"

"I don't know where he is right now, but his name is Tim

Sherman."

"You mean Ace," Roger, the shortstop said excitedly. "He's the best pitcher in the league! Maybe we'll finally win a game."

"Maybe we will with Ace Sherman pitching in Pete's place," I smiled.

"Ace Sherman," Joey, the catcher sneered. "How could you pick him to play on our team after what he did to Pete? I think he beaned him on purpose because he was jealous of Pete. Pete was a good pitcher."

"That's exactly the kind of attitude I don't want on this team. Ace did not, I repeat, did not bean Pete on purpose. Ace is going to have a hard enough time adjusting to a new team. I'm sure he doesn't want to be here any more than some of you don't want him here. Like Roger said before, maybe with Ace on our team, we can get into the win column and hopefully make a run for the playoffs."

"I didn't say that," Roger said confused. "I said..."

"It doesn't matter," I interrupted. "What matters is that with the acquisition of Ace to our team, not only do we have the best pitcher in the league, other than you Mike, but we also have nine players. It's either Ace or forfeit. Remember that."

"So, does that mean we have to be nice to him?" Joey the catcher added. "Personally, I can't stand the kid. He's too cocky if you ask me."

"You, Joey, of all people, should try to get along with him, you being the catcher," I scolded. "I don't want any hard feelings between you guys. When you signed up into this league, it was for one reason. Can anybody tell me why you joined baseball?"

"Yeah," Luke, the third baseman, laughed. "To get out of doing homework."

"Very funny, Luke," I said smiling but then gave him a sneer. "You're lucky we only have nine players or I'd make you sit the bench for a comment like that. But seriously, does anybody know why we go out of our way to show up for practices, why we use what we've learned on game day, and give it our all?"

"Because we hate soccer," Luke snickered.

"Luke, that's enough out of you," I wanted to laugh but tried to be sincere. "Does anybody know? Now be serious."

"Because we love to play baseball," John, the center fielder, squeaked out.

"Exactly!" I raised my voice, startling the players. "And why do we love baseball? Because it's fun," I answered quickly before Luke could think of a wise remark. "We're here to have fun."

"It sure would be a lot more fun if we won a game," Gary, the left fielder, added.

"Sure, winning is fun," I pointed out. "But we've come so close to winning many of our games. You can't look at a win-loss record to decide if you're having fun. Take for instance the day Joey went four for four at bat. Then he picked off a guy trying to steal second base. Then, if not for a bad call by the umpire, he would've stopped the game-winning run at home plate. I'll bet people were talking about that play for a couple of weeks. Now, Joey, you've got to admit. Didn't you have fun in that game even though we lost?"

"Yeah, but that umpire needs glasses," Joey smiled. "I had

him out by a mile."

"I agree, but the ump made a bad call. It's just another part of the game we all love."

"Love," Luke snapped his head back, "you loved that bad call by the ump?"

"No, but the other team sure did. Did you see their faces when the ump called him safe? Those faces could have been ours if the ump yelled, 'He's out of there!' That's what I'm trying to tell you. We could've won that game, but we didn't, but we had fun. That's what I want you kids to do the rest of the season, to have plain and simple fun."

"Are we done talking, Coach?" Luke said rubbing his leg. "My leg fell asleep."

"Just one last thing, if and when Ace does arrive, treat him with a little respect. Try and make him feel welcome because I'm sure being traded took a little fun out of the game for him. Try and keep that in mind. I'm sure some of you guys have friends or have made new friends on this team. How would any of you feel if you were traded to another team?"

"If I were traded to the Newport Sneaks, I wouldn't mind," Luke laughed. "At least I'd be on a winning team."

"Then I guess you wouldn't mind giving me five laps around the field since you're still on my team. And I hope you have fun doing them, wise guy."

"But, Coach," Luke pleaded. "I was only kidding."

"Well, I'm not," I raised my voice. "And if I see you walking at any time, I'll make you start all over."

"That's not fair," Luke sneered throwing his glove against the dugout fence.

"That just cost you an extra lap," I concluded. "Now get running."

Practice began to wind down on a dismal note. Ace had never shown up, and I was disappointed not to see how the other players would react to him after my speech in the dugout. I felt I was wasting my time with Ace and had to get things settled before our next game. That night I called the Sherman residence and spoke with Mrs. Sherman.

"Mrs. Sherman," I greeted, then introduced myself. "I'm Tim's new coach Cecil Blake. Do you know why Tim never showed up for practice tonight? I wanted him to get acquainted with his new team."

"I didn't know anything about it," she said surprised. "Tim never mentioned anything to me. My husband usually handles such matters but he's been out of town on business. He usually informs me if I'm to bring Tim to practice. That's strange that neither of them said a word."

"Is there any way I could speak with Tim? We have a game tomorrow night at 5:30 and I want to be sure he'll be there. I was going to give him a schedule and a uniform, but like I said before, he never showed up for practice tonight."

"At the moment, he's not in right now," she added. "But he did leave the house with his baseball glove. Maybe he's pitching to our neighbor, Eddie. Those two boys practice together almost every day. Can I have Tim call you back?"

"That would be great. My number is 555-1958. Please tell him it's important that he contacts me tonight. I'll make sure I stay home so I don't miss his call."

"I'll give Tim the message. I'm sorry if he's caused you any inconvenience."

When Tim never returned my call, I became angry. But when Tim never showed up for the game, I became furious. I felt like I had let my team down. All the other eight players had shown up with a hope to win only to fall to zero and eight by forfeit. Instead of calling Tim's house on the phone, I decided to make a personal appearance. I wasn't going to let Tim dodge me any longer.

I stormed up the long sidewalk that led to the Sherman's home and gave the wooden door three hard knocks. As my knuckles throbbed, I realized I had to control my temper.

A man's voice yelled from behind the door, "Eddie, what are you trying to do, knock down the door?" Then the door swung open and there stood the towering Mr. Sherman. His once stern voice turned frail and apologetic, "Oh, I'm sorry. I thought you were the neighbor's kid. Can I help you?"

"I apologize for knocking so hard," I said embarrassed. "I'm Cecil Blake, Tim's new coach. This is the Sherman's residence I hope?"

"Yes it is, and I'm John Sherman, Timothy's dad," he introduced. "What seems to be the problem?"

"I'm not quite sure. It would appear that Tim has quit the league but is doing it in a roundabout way. The day I spoke to him after the trade he seemed okay with the idea, but he never showed up for practice. Last night I left a message with your wife to have him call me, and he never called me back. We ended up forfeiting tonight's game due to the lack of players. I need to know if he's going to play because I need another player. It's not fair to the other players to keep on forfeiting."

"No, it's not," Mr. Sherman agreed. "I was unaware that Tim was being so negligent. Please come in so we can get to the bottom of this hide and seek game. Have a seat in the living room. Tim's upstairs in his room. I'll go get him."

Ace reluctantly strolled into the living room with his head bowed down, staring at the carpet. His parents shadowed behind him showing embarrassment and anger on both their faces. I rose from my seat forcing a smile from my tense face to greet Mrs. Sherman. I had hoped to relieve this uncomfortable setting through the art of conversation and a smile.

"Hello, Mrs. Sherman. You're even lovelier than your voice on the phone. It's so nice to finally meet you."

"Why, thank you," she said blushing. "I'd just like to apologize to you and your team for forfeiting tonight's game. I had no idea Tim was still playing ball. After I spoke with you on the phone, I gave Tim your message and he told me he was quitting the team," she paused and glared over at Tim, raising her voice. "Isn't that true Tim?"

Tim was speechless.

"Tim!" Mr. Sherman hollered. "Answer your mother!"

"Yes," Tim muttered. "I said I was quitting."

"And, Tim," her voice grew louder. "Didn't I also tell you it was up to you to call Coach Blake and let him know you were quitting his team? Why didn't you call him? You told me you did."

"So you lied to your mother," Mr. Sherman took a step forward and spun Tim around. "Look at me when I'm talking to you! I'm not on the floor! So you're a quitter and a liar," Mr. Sherman's eyes widened. "What next?"

"Why can't I just play on my regular team?" Tim began sobbing. "Why was it me that had to be traded?"

"Because of the rules," Mr. Sherman yelled. "The league made a decision which left you with a decision. It's quite simple. You either play for Coach Blake or you end your season."

"Excuse me, but," I interrupted feeling sorry for Tim. "Maybe there's another solution. Maybe another player from the Newport Sneaks will volunteer to take Tim's place on my roster. I mean, if playing for Coach Newport means that much to him, I won't stand in his way. I can call for a special meeting with Coach

Newport and the commissioner."

"I appreciate your compassion, Mr. Blake, but Tim has got to learn to respect the decisions of his peers," Mr. Sherman said straightforward. "Things like this happen every day in life and you can't just ignore or lie your way out of them. So what's it going to be, Tim? Play for Coach Blake or quit?"

Ace began to sob uncontrollably, trying to catch his breath. I felt that even if Ace had joined my team, his heart wouldn't be in the sport any longer. If only Mr. Newport could see the trouble he caused with his roster tampering. We all became innocent bystanders in a businessman's greed and awaited the fate of a young boy's decision.

"So what's it gonna be Tim?" Mr. Sherman demanded an answer. "I'm sure Coach Blake has better things to do than to chase you down for an answer."

"I'll, i'll," Ace stuttered, wiping away his tears. "I'll play."

I let out a relieved sigh and rubbed Ace on the top of his head knowing he made the right choice.

"Now, don't you think you owe Coach Blake an apology?" Mrs. Sherman insisted.

"That won't be necessary, Ace," I said feeling enough harm was done. "Just show up for practice on Saturday. We've got another game on Monday."

"He'll be there," Mr. Sherman guaranteed. "I'll personally see to that. So what time will practice be?"

"Oh, gee, that would be nice to let you know, it's at 9:30 am. Sorry to create such a fuss."

"If anyone should apologize, it should be me," said Mrs. Sherman. "I should have made sure that Tim had called you when I learned that he was quitting. I'm glad that he didn't. Thank you for stopping over, and we're sorry for any misunderstanding."

"It was a pleasure meeting you both. I'll see you on Saturday, Tim. Goodnight."

Skip Freeman suddenly broke into the conversation saying, "And people think when it comes to coaching, it's just going over baseball fundamentals with the kids and shuffling around a lineup. I guess you have to be part public relations officer too."

"Yes, and part babysitter, part taxi cab driver, and the list goes on," Coach Blake laughed.

"So with Ace in the lineup, how did that first game turn out?"

"Not as well as one might think. It takes more than one player to turn a team around," Coach Blake added. "We still had a lot of bugs to work out with our infielders and there were many mixed emotions from everyone involved in Ace's first game with Mary's Dress Barn, right Ace?"

"I'll say," Ace started to speak but was abruptly halted by Skip.

"Before we go any further with this, it's time for another break. We'll be right back after this."

A Strange Turn of Events

"We're at the midpoint of SNN's exclusive interview with Tim "The Ace" Sherman," Skip Freeman announced. "Before the break, Ace was about to tell us about his first game with his new team in the ABYL." Skip turned to Ace and said, "At the time, you were only twelve years old, and you were traded from an undefeated team to a winless team. Can you tell our young viewers in the audience what your hardest transition was adapting to your new team?"

"I think the hardest thing for me at the time was getting my head back into the game," Ace pointed out. "I was in a situation I didn't want to be in. I didn't like Coach Blake and held a grudge against him. I felt it was his fault I had been traded and was being forced to play on his team. I didn't know any of the players seeing how I boycotted my first practice and game, and when I decided to finally go to a practice, it was rained out. I had no desire to be on the playing field, and for the first time in my life, I couldn't wait for the season to end. To make matters worse, during my first game with my new team, my former team, the Newport Sneaks was playing in the adjacent field that very same day."

Ace began to tell what happened that day in vivid detail.

"Okay, guys," Coach Blake said with enthusiasm. "We're the home team, so we take the field first. I've got a good feeling about this game. It's time to turn the season around. Everybody take your positions. Mike, you're pitching the first three innings so, Ace, you'll be playing right field. Let's have some fun."

I stood in shallow right field watching our pitcher warm up and he was terrible. One out of every four pitches managed to cross the plate. Joey, the catcher, spent more time chasing the ball to the backstop than he actually did catching.

Our infielders weren't much better. During the infield warmup, Nick, the first baseman, threw a grounder to Luke on third. Luke picked up the ball and threw an off-balanced throw back to first. After his release of the ball, Luke hunched up his shoulders as if to guide the ball so it wouldn't hit the pitcher in the head. Fortunately, it barely missed him and bounced in front of Nick, grazing him in the shin.

Nick sat on the first base bag, rubbing his shin, and threw a weak grounder to Roger, the short stop. Instead of charging the ball like in a bunt situation, Roger patiently waited for the ball to roll into his glove. If he were on Coach Newport's team, Coach Newport would be having a screaming fit. Instead, Coach Blake encouraged him by telling him what a good catch he had made. It was no wonder this team was winless.

A ball hitting my leg drew my attention to John, the center fielder.

"Nice catch!" John yelled followed by a laugh. "Quit daydreaming and warm up."

Angered by his remark, I picked up the ball and hurled it back to him as hard as I could. He fearfully stepped out of the ball's path, and I yelled, "What are you, afraid of the ball? No wonder the coach stuck you in the outfield."

"Balls in," the umpire yelled.

"Coming down," Joey warned Ted on second for his upcoming throw.

The game was about to begin. Mike, the pitcher overthrew Joey at home plate and hit the umpire in the chest pad with a loud thud. Joey retrieved the ball and tossed it shy of the shortstop who was covering second base. The ball bounced between his legs and sped past Ted, who was supposed to be backing up the throw. Eventually, the ball trickled over to John in center field, who was busy swatting at a butterfly with his glove.

"John," I yelled shaking my head. "Get the ball!"

"C'mon, guys," Coach Blake shouted from the dugout. "You can do better than that!"

Needless to say, it was going to be a long game. As I stood in right field, I watched Mike walk the first seven batters. It was four to nothing with no outs and no hits yet. I wanted so badly to take the mound that I was almost willing to push Mike off of it. I looked over at Coach Blake waved my glove in the air and pointed to myself. He ignored my silent plea to take the mound and paced back and forth hoping Mike would find his strike zone. When Mike had walked the ninth batter, I slapped my hands in frustration against my hips. Out of desperation, I clasped my hands together in the air and prayed that he'd throw it down the strike zone.

I flinched when I heard the pinging sound of the ball colliding with the aluminum bat. It was a well-hit ball that sent me back peddling to the fence. As I leaped up as high as I could, I could feel the ball graze the tip of my glove, and when I squeezed my mitt together, I knew I had come up empty. The ball disappeared out of sight into the tall grass as the other team rounded the bases for a grand slam home run.

I flung my glove to the ground and gave it a swift kick, sending it tumbling away from me. When I looked up, I saw the other team celebrating and noticed Coach Blake waving us into the dugout. I took my time on my way off the field and was unaware as to what was happening. We never got a single player out, yet the other team was taking the field.

Once I returned to the dugout, I immediately asked, "Coach, what's going on? How come they're out on the field?"

"It's the ten batter rule," he said like it was something his team was used to. He then turned to Mike who was obviously shaken. "Don't worry about it, Mike," he said with compassion. "That's just the kind of pitch I want you to throw next inning, smack-dab over the plate."

"But they just got a grand slam," I said inconsiderately. "If he keeps that up, we'll never get anyone out."

"And if you caught the ball, it would have been an out," Coach Blake encouraged.

"So, what are you saying," I blasted back. "That it was my fault because I couldn't jump high enough?"

"I'm not blaming anyone," Coach Blake became annoyed. "I'm merely letting Mike know that if he pitches the ball over the plate and they hit it, he has eight other players in the field to get the runner out. That's why baseball is called a team sport."

"You call this a team," I insulted. "We're losing ten to nothing after half an inning."

"That's enough out of you," Coach Blake yelled. "I was talking to Mike, not you. Go sit down and root for your team. Okay. Who's up at bat?"

"Luke, John, then Joey," Mrs. Blake read off the lineup sheet.

"Okay, Luke, you've been hot lately, let's see some hitting out there," Coach Blake encouraged. "This game isn't over yet. Let's go!"

The game progressed into being one of the most lopsided games of the season. After three innings, the score was 23 to 1, but Coach Blake was talking as if we had the lead.

"Okay, Ace," Coach Blake said, resting his hand on my shoulder. "Maybe if you can shut them down this inning our guys will get back into the game. Let's see what you've got."

As I picked up my glove to exit the dugout, a young boy with a cast on his right thumb blocked my way out. His face seemed familiar, but I couldn't recall where I had seen him before.

"Hey Peter-Peter-pumpkin eater. How's the thumb?" Coach Blake asked, happy to see him.

"It's still a little sore," he said trying to bend his thumb. "The cast comes off in a couple of weeks."

"That's great, but what are you doing over here? Are you lost? Your new team is playing in the other field. I would think that Coach Newport would've let you coach first base to keep you involved in the game."

"He yells too much, so I quit the team. I'm an injured free agent now." Pete grinned.

"So you quit," Coach Blake seemed disappointed. "That's too bad."

"I can't play anymore, so what's the sense?"

"Well, you can always learn by watching, you know."

"Not on that team. It's like a shouting match for professional wrestling. If I ever had to play on his team, I wouldn't make it through spring training. I would quit before the season started."

85

"Excuse me, Coach," I interrupted. "But I have to get on the pitching mound and go warm up."

"Hey Pete, you know Ace, don't you? He took over your spot as pitcher." Coach Blake informed him, and that's when I realized who Pete actually was.

"I know his fast ball better than I know him," Pete replied. "Nice to meet you."

"Hey, I'm sorry about your thumb," I apologized. "That pitch just got away from me."

"You know something, when I realized I was about to get hit, I froze up like a deer in front of an oncoming car. Luckily, at the last second, I moved my head out of the way. My thumb hurts bad enough. I can't imagine getting hit in the head with your fastball. You've got a strong arm."

"Thanks but, I don't mean to be rude, but I have to go warm up my arm. I hope your thumb gets better soon."

"I'm sure it will. I have a whole year to get back in shape.

Anyway, you better get out there. The team is waiting."

I stood on the mound and the feel of the ball in my hand was a welcomed one. As I warmed up my arm with Joey the catcher, I threw eight strikes with eight pitches and was ready for the first batter.

"Play ball!" the umpire shouted, and a strange thing happened to me when the batter took his stance. I imagined Coach Newport from behind the backstop. His arms were raised and his fingers were curled within the chain-link fence. I looked the batter in the eye and then at the image of Coach Newport before my windup.

Coach Newport's image gave a sinister grin as he tugged on his left ear with his right hand and slowly dragged his finger across his throat. My pitch bounced off the batter's helmet and the crowd gasped at the sight of him falling to the ground. A round of applause echoed across the field when the injured batter rose to his feet and trotted over to first base. I looked back behind the backstop and the image of Coach Newport had disappeared.

I rubbed my eyes, trying to regain focus, as the next batter took a couple of practice swings before he stepped into the batter's box. When I started my windup, the batter stepped back to call a time out in order to adjust his batting glove. That's when the image of Coach Newport reappeared from behind the backstop.

I closed my eyes hoping that when I opened them, his image would be gone. That didn't happen. Again, his right hand tugged on his left ear and his finger slowly dragged across his throat.

"No," I yelled, letting the ball fly and caught the batter in the thigh.

"Boo," the crowd moaned.

"Get him off the mound before he hurts somebody," a father yelled.

"Time out!" Coach Blake cried out and motioned me over to him at the first base line. "What's the problem, Ace? You feel okay?"

"I don't know what's wrong with me," I confessed. "This never happened to me before."

"Just take your time," Coach Blake consoled me. "Just aim for Joey's glove."

"Okay, Coach," I said, checking behind the backstop. "He's gone now. I think I'll be all right."

"Who's gone?" Coach Blake said puzzled. "What are you talking about?"

"Never mind, I'm okay," I said disillusioned and walked back to the pitcher's mound.

"Play ball!" the umpire cried out, and once again Coach Newport materialized.

Like before, his signal was given, but this time I would aim for Coach Newport. I hurled the ball with all my might and it lodged into the diamond-shaped webbing of the fence. The ball was stuck at eye level of Coach Newport, and he appeared to poke it free with his finger. I watched the ball drop to the ground as Joey scrambled back from my wild pitch. Meanwhile, the runners were advancing, stealing second and third base.

I took a deep breath and decided to concentrate on only one thing, Joey's glove. I was afraid to look anywhere past the umpire. As I made my windup, I visualized Coach Newport as the umpire. The umpire tugged on his left ear with his right hand and slowly dragged his finger across his throat. I threw the ball thinking he was Coach Newport, and it bounced off his face mask.

"My time!" the umpire yelled and made his way to the dugout to speak with Coach Blake. The next thing I knew, Coach Blake shouted, "Luke, you take the mound. Ace, you're on third."

"This is turning out to be a ghost story rather than a baseball story," Skip Freeman interrupted. "It's hard to believe that Ace was able to continue playing baseball with that ghost haunting him from behind the backstop."

"It took some time before Ace could rid himself of his psychological fears. When that took place, only Ace could answer that question," Coach Blake added. "But after that game, it was me who was taking the heat from all the parents and my co-workers."

"In what way?" Skip asked confused. "It would appear that

Ace had the problem and not you."

"You see, that same night, the Newport Sneaks only won their game by one run. That game ended long before ours and some curious fans came to watch Ace pitch, knowing he always closes the game. When they saw him playing at third base, they thought I was a bad coach for not having him pitch. None of them realized what had taken place that night.

After our game ended, I remember being approached by another coach who had just lost to the Newport Sneaks. He was a co-worker of mine and was the head of the Personnel Department. He was the man who hired me for my production control job, and I welcomed his arrival. What he told me that night, I found very disturbing."

"Hey, Mr. Preston," I greeted. "How did your team do against the unbeatable Newport Sneaks?"

"We lost," he said unconcerned. "But we easily could have won. I didn't want to be the one that stops Newport's win streak. I like my job at the sneaker plant."

"And what exactly do you mean by that?"

"Don't be so ignorant," he sneered. "If my team beat his tonight, I'd be alongside your buddy, Bruce Rogers in the unemployment line. As a matter of fact, if you weren't doing such a fine job with production control, you'd be out of a job for stealing Ace from his team."

"Did I hear you right? Did you say that Bruce Rogers was fired?" I was shocked. "When did this happen?"

"Today," he said unsympathetic. "They made him clean out his desk and security escorted him out the door. I'm surprised you didn't hear about it."

"This is news to me. What did he do to get fired?" I asked.

"I guess he overlooked something in the books and the company ended up losing a lot of money because of it. He's an accountant and he must've placed a decimal point in the wrong spot. I don't know for sure. The one thing I do know is that he doesn't work at the Newport Sneaker plant anymore."

"I wonder if his involvement in the trading of Ace to my team had anything to do with him being fired."

"You never know. You don't want to step on Mr. Newport's toes. He should've just let Ace stay on Newport's team and never should've gotten the state commissioner involved. I know I wouldn't have. That was his first mistake."

"But you don't know the whole story. There was a conflict of interest involved. He had to go to the state commissioner."

"Apparently Mr. Newport didn't see it that way. Now Mr. Roger's main interest will be to find a new job. Quite stupid on his part, I would say."

"This whole win streak record is really getting out of control. I feel like it's my fault that Bruce was fired."

"Well, there's nothing you can do about it now. What's done is done."

Anyway, I see you had Ace playing third base tonight. What did your team do, run up the score so high that you didn't pitch Ace?

So, you finally won a game."

"I wish," I said discouraged. "We got killed tonight. I don't even know what the final score was. I lost track after the fourth inning."

"Do you mean to tell me that you went through all the trouble to get Ace on your team and you stuck him on third base? Where did you learn how to coach?"

"I had him pitch, but if you saw him bean the first two batters, I don't think you would've left him on the mound. I think he was rusty or something, it just wasn't his night. He wouldn't have made a difference anyway. We were down by almost twenty runs. I took him out for the safety of the other players."

"You should've given him another chance. Ace is the best."

"Well, tonight he wasn't. Something is bothering Ace and it's affecting his pitching. I'm not sure what his problem is, but I have an idea what it might be. I'll have to sit him down and talk it over with him."

"Maybe it's the team he's on," Mr. Preston insulted. "He's used to being on a winning club. He stands little chance of winning with your team."

"Well, we play your team sometime next week," I defended. "Maybe that'll be the game we put everything together and win."

"I doubt it," he said snapping his head back. "Especially if you keep playing Ace on third base. You won't stand a chance."

"I guess we'll find out next week on the playing field. I'll see you then. I really have to get going. I'm starving."

"I'll see you sooner than that, or did you forget?" he pointed out. "Friday night is ABYL night at the church bazaar. I thought you and your wife volunteered to work one of the game booths."

"Where does the time go? I completely forgot about that. I think after this baseball season is over, I'm going to take a long vacation on some island where they've never heard of baseball."

"I think if someone snaps Mr. Newport's win streak, you'll be on a permanent vacation along with Mr. Rogers. Newport's team isn't the same without Ace. I could have beaten him tonight but to keep my job, I closed the game with my worst pitcher and still almost won. It was my way of showing Mr. Newport that I'm a team player."

"So you could have won but didn't by changing your lineup. And you call me a bad coach? Don't you care about how the kids feel? I feel sorry for that kid you put in to close the game. He probably knew he shouldn't have closed the game and became the goat. I'm sure he's being teased by all the other kids on the team for losing. I can't believe you would put a kid in that kind of position."

"He'll get over it. I let him know after the game that he did his best. He seemed all right with it. No real harm done."

"If you say so Mr. Preston, but when you play my team next week, you better be prepared."

"Don't worry," he boasted. "If you think you had trouble keeping track of the score tonight, wait till you play my team. Mark my words. Once Mr. Newport's win streak is broken, I'll be after the championship trophy next season."

"Sure you will . . . that is if Mr. Newport lets you."

"Whatever," he muttered and he turned his back to me, making his way off the field.

"Sorry to interrupt," Skip Freeman broke into the story. "But now it's time for our boss to say a few words. Stay tuned and we'll be right back after this commercial."

Isn't Life Bizarre?

"Hi, and welcome back to SNN's exclusive interview with Tim "The Ace" Sherman. I'm Skip Freeman, and if you're just tuning in, we found a point in Ace Sherman's career where he seemed to be falling apart. It appeared that the trading of this young athlete back in his early days of the ABYL wreaked havoc in his mind. He began imagining his former coach behind the backstop and was unable to throw a pitch over home plate. I think the only thing that kept Ace from sitting the bench was the fact that his new team only had nine players, which was the main reason he was traded.

What I think most of our viewing audience would like to know is, when did the magic of pitching come back to him and what helped Ace shake that image of his former coach from behind the backstop? Care to answer that for us, Ace?"

"I'd be glad to, Skip," Ace said sincerely. "You know, life can be funny at times. Sometimes, quite bizarre. It's strange how you can discover things to change your life in the least expected places."

Ace leaned back comfortably in his chair and began to explain what happened that night long ago.

I remember being at the church bazaar that Friday night. It was ABYL night and everybody from the league was there to help raise money for new equipment. A small portion of Friday night's profit would be donated to the ABYL equipment fund. I was by myself and felt depressed as I walked aimlessly through the crowd. I was still thinking about my hallucinations behind the backstop and I didn't think I'd ever find the courage to take the mound again. I felt my career as a pitcher was over.

My attention was caught when a familiar voice pierced the crowd noise. It was Coach Blake's voice and he was working one of the most popular game booths. I was surprised not to see a crowd gathered in front of the booth and stopped in my tracks not wanting to be seen by Coach Blake. I figured he would lecture me about my last game, and I wasn't in any mood to discuss it.

"C'mon, step right up!" Coach Blake yelled out. "Knock over three dolls and win a prize. Three tries for a dollar," he encouraged but no one paid him any mind.

I ducked behind an elderly couple who shielded me from his view, and when the time was right, I bolted for the game booth next to his. The noise from the rapid-fire BB gun startled me, and I watched a man attempt to shoot out the large red circle on the target. He failed to win a prize and walked away disgusted, so I laid a dollar down for my chance.

The attendant filled the BB gun with ammunition and then stepped aside. As I took aim at the red spot on the target, I became distracted with the sound of Coach Blake's voice.

"Hey, Bruce," he yelled above the merry-go-round music, "Bruce Rogers," and he waved him over with his hand.

I refocused on the target and squeezed the trigger. The BB's blurted out in one quick rush and penetrated the paper. Fragments fell down like leaves from a tree, and in an instant, the gun had emptied. A slight ringing in my ear was followed by a brief silence as the attendant retrieved the mangled target.

"Sorry, kid. You lose," the attendant announced. "Your aim is a little off. Care to try again?"

I shook my head no and stepped aside for the next contestant. I leaned against the edge of the game booth daydreaming and couldn't help overhearing Coach Blake's conversation with Mr. Rogers.

"So, Bruce, tell me what happened," Coach Blake said uneasy. "Why did Mr. Newport fire you?"

"I've been asking myself that question for the last few days and still haven't figured it out," he said bewildered. "The whole incident wasn't even my fault."

"What wasn't your fault?"

"Well, to make a long story short, it turned out that one of the new employees in my accounting department made a major error with one of the company's important accounts. Then Newport calls me into his office and starts screaming at me. 'How come you didn't catch this error? That's why you're the head of your department, to make sure your staff doesn't screw up!' Then he fired me. He didn't even give me a chance to explain that I was out sick that day the error occurred."

"Well, why didn't you explain that to him?" Coach Blake asked.

"Because every time I tried to, he would interrupt by saying, 'I don't have time for excuses. Now, get out.' So I left his office knowing he wouldn't listen."

"So, now what will you do for a job?" Coach Blake asked. "And how is your wife handling your loss?"

"At first she was disappointed because by losing my job, I also lost my medical benefits. As far as finding another job, right now I'm bargaining with two different accounting firms to see who will make me the best offer. Whoever can give me the best medical insurance is where I aim to go."

"That's a smart move when you have kids. All it takes is an unexpected illness and your whole life turns upside down. Half your paycheck can end up going toward hospital bills. I know that situation all too well. I'm still paying for when my son was in the hospital, and that was over two years ago."

"You have a son?" Mr. Rogers asked unaware. "How come

I've never met him?"

"Terry passed away two years ago at the age of nine," Coach Blake told him as his eyes became swollen with tears. "He had an incurable blood disease."

"I'm so sorry," Mr. Rogers frowned. "I guess the loss of my job is nothing compared to what you must've gone through. I don't know how I'd ever get over the loss of a child."

"You never really get over it. There's always something that happens during the course of the day to remind me of Terry and how much I miss him. I'll never forget him."

"I'm sure you won't," Mr. Rogers sighed and briefly paused, being lost for words. "I guess I'll go see if I can round up my wife and kids. I'll see you around."

"Hey, before you go," Coach Blake returned to his cheerful self. "Could you do me one favor?"

"Sure Cecil, what do you need?"

"I need you to knock over three of these dolls with three of these balls," Coach Blake smiled. "But it will cost you a buck."

"Sure, Cecil," Mr. Rogers smiled back. "I'll give it a try."

Mr. Rogers missed all three tosses and to my surprise Coach Blake shouted out, "And we have a winner!" He took three stuffed monkeys from off the prize shelf and tossed them over to Mr. Rogers.

With a puzzled stare, Mr. Rogers asked, "But I thought the object of the game was to knock over the dolls, not miss them."

"It is," Coach Blake pointed out. "But at the rate this booth is going, those will be the only prizes I hand out tonight."

"Now that you mention it, I'm surprised that this booth isn't crowded by now. This is usually one of the most popular games here."

"I don't know what it is," Coach Blake wondered. "It's like I've got the plague or something. No one wants to come near me. I don't know what I did to these people."

"Maybe since I was fired, people are afraid to associate with you because they think they might lose their jobs too. To be honest with you, I think the real reason I was fired was because of my involvement with you getting Ace Sherman on your team."

"I think you're right, Bruce, but we'll never know for sure," Coach Blake concluded. "You better go find the rest of your family before they spend all your money. I'll see you later."

Mr. Rogers grinned and then nodded, but as he turned away, he bumped into Mrs. Blake. The hamburger she was carrying pressed against her dress and then fell to the ground.

"Nice going, Bruce," Coach Blake kidded. "You walk as well as you throw."

"I'm sorry, ma'am," Mr. Rogers apologized. "I'll get you another hamburger."

"Oh, that's quite all right," she said checking her dress for any ketchup stains. "My husband could stand to lose a little weight."

"Now that you nearly knocked my wife over," Coach Blake laughed. "I may as well introduce you to her. Betty, I'd like you to meet the clumsy Bruce Rogers. He's the ABYL commissioner and former bookkeeper at the Newport Sneaker plant. Betty is my wife and team manager."

"Nice bumping into you," Mr. Rogers joked and shook her hand. "Now let me go get you another hamburger."

"That's all right, Bruce," Coach Blake interrupted. "I have to get out of this game booth so the league can make some money. Betty, you take over while I put a real money making scheme to work."

"But where are you going?" she asked confused. "We volunteered for this booth."

"I'll be over at the dunk tank," Coach Blake grinned. "With my popularity, I'm sure I'll be able to draw a crowd. I'll make some money for the league."

"Okay, dear," Betty Blake told him. "But be careful."

"I'll be careful," he said with sarcasm. "I'll wear a life jacket so I won't drown."

Overhearing that conversation brought about a big change in the way I felt toward Coach Blake. I actually started to like him. At the time, I didn't know what had happened to cause everyone to dislike him or why Mr. Rogers was fired, but I felt it had something to do with me. I was curious to see how the crowd would react to him being the main attraction at the dunk tank and would wait until he was out of sight before following him over to the dunk tank.

I watched him weave his way through the crowd and when I thought there was no chance of him spotting me, I left the BB gun booth to follow him. I stood on the outskirts; close enough to hear what was being said yet far enough away where he wouldn't notice me.

Above the tank was a sign which read, "Three Pitches for a Dollar. Three Strikes and You're Out!" Coach Blake slowly crept up onto the perch and dabbed his toe into the water shrugging his shoulders in a shiver. His eyes peered out into the crowd, searching for a contestant.

"Hey!" he shouted out to the flowing crowd. "Anybody out there good enough to dunk me? I surely doubt it."

Most people looked up and then away and ignored him. It was obvious that no one wanted to have anything to do with him, even if it meant dunking him in a drum of cold water. That didn't discourage him though, and he changed his game plan of heckling the whole crowd to picking on just one individual. His eyes scanned the mob of people until he found an unsuspecting victim carrying a plate of fried chicken.

"Hey, fowl mouth!" he yelled as many people turned toward him. "Yeah, you eating the chicken," he singled out a man who suddenly stopped. "You know what they say, don't you? That you are what you eat, you big chicken. Why don't you wipe the grease off your mouth and show everyone what a man you could be and try and dunk me. Or are you a chicken?" Coach Blake tucked his hands under his armpits and flapped his arms like wings, then clucked like a chicken.

"What are you, a screwball?" the puzzled man blurted back as he waived him off with his hand and walked away from Coach Blake's continuous clucking.

Coach Blake was starting to have fun. It was evident by the

smile that had beamed across his face. He didn't seem to care what a fool he made of himself because no one seemed to like him anyway. His head flinched about with quick repetitious jerks as a chicken would as he looked for his next victim. He crowed like a rooster when he eyed the unsuspecting Mr. Rogers.

"Now there's a man with a throwing arm!" Coach Blake shouted out, pointing at Mr. Rogers. "Hey, Bruce, my grandmother throws better than you and she has arthritis. C'mon, Mr. Rogers. Why don't you take that sweater off and show us what you've got?"

Mr. Rogers stood by his wife and three children feeling embarrassed. He shyly shook his head no and whispered something to his wife. He gave a quick wave goodbye and tried to exit the area but Coach Blake continued his ranting.

"Where are you going, you pencil pushing mamas' boy? Stop hiding behind your wife's skirt and lay your money down. Three pitches for a dollar. Three strikes and you're out."

Mr. Rogers turned to his wife with a half-witted grin and then shook his head. A crowd began to form in front of the dunk tank as a young boy cried out, "Dunk him!"

Mrs. Rogers opened her purse and slid out a one dollar bill. She shook it in front of his face, egging him on. With a quick swipe of his hand, he reluctantly snagged the bill and slammed it down on the plywood counter.

"Okay, funny boy," Mr. Rogers yelled back with a threat. "Be prepared to get wet."

Coach Blake pretended to yawn, showing no fear of getting dunked. He calmly turned to the dunk tank assistant and pretended to whisper. He cupped both hands around his mouth then surprised everyone by shouting, "Give the man only two balls, he doesn't know how to count. He's the only accountant I know that works with his socks off so he can count to twenty."

"Keep it up, Blake," Mr. Rogers said cupping the ball in his hands like a major league pitcher. "You're starting to make me mad."

"Ooh, now I'm scared. There's nothing worse than a mad accountant. What are you going to do, dunk me or divide me? Now throw the darn ball."

Mr. Rogers took aim while Coach Blake grimaced, anticipating a sudden plunge. The ball hit the canvas backstop with an empty thump.

"Wow, what a breeze," Coach Blake heckled. "I won't need to get wet to cool myself off with all this wind blowing about. So how many balls do you have left, Mr. Accountant? You started with three and you missed by a mile with one, now that leaves you with how many?" He paused, "Take your time. You can use a calculator if you can't figure it out in your head. I can wait."

Wanting to get out of the spotlight of the growing crowd's attention, Mr. Rogers hurled both balls knowing he was out of his league. He was no match for Coach Blake and his heckling and missed his next two throws. He stepped away from the table somewhat humiliated but he knew Coach Blake needed someone to get the crowd involved. He knew it was harmless fun.

"C'mon," Mr. Rogers yelled to the crowd. "Somebody dunk this windbag."

"Yeah, c'mon you bunch of turkeys," Coach Blake felt the crowd becoming excited. "I'm still dry, so who's next?"

Everyone looked at each other as if they'd be the one to step up to the challenge but nobody did. It was now once again up to Coach Blake to single someone out.

"Anybody?" his eyes scanned the crowd until someone caught his attention. "Hey you, Coach Preston. Let's see how you can handle the kind of pressure you put on your kids on the playing field, Mr. Champion-wanna-be."

"I don't want to embarrass you," he insulted. "You're already washed up as a coach. You don't need me to give you a bath by dunking you. Go pick on somebody else."

"But, Coach Preston," he returned. "Aren't you the head of the Personnel Department at the Newport Sneaker plant? Did anybody fill that job as head coach for your team after you put in a rookie pitcher against the Newport Sneaks when your team had a chance to win? That was a bad call by a rookie coach if you ask me. Any good coaches apply?" There was a calm of anticipation in the crowd. "Three pitches for a dollar, Coach Preston. Three strikes and you're out. Lay your money down and donate toward the league, Coach Preston, and dunk me if you can."

Mr. Preston squinted one eye in anger but he wanted to walk away. Unwanted pressure soon became a factor.

"Dunk him, Daddy," his six-year-old son encouraged.

"Go for it, Hon'," his wife stood up for him. "I wouldn't take that from that loser. Dunk him!"

"Yeah, honey-pie. Dunk the loser," Coach Blake antagonized. "Let's see your underarm granny's pitch. I haven't seen that one in years, honey-pie."

"That does it, Blake," Coach Preston growled. "You're going down. Give me a ball!"

"Okay, Coach. You know the rules. First do some stretching exercises before you throw. I wouldn't want you to pull a muscle. It looks like your stomach muscle is pretty much pulled. It's hanging over your belt. You can skip that stomach warm up. Just loosen up your arm for now. We don't have that much time. People are waiting to watch you fail."

Coach Preston hurled the ball with an agonizing grunt and hit the canvas backstop with a wallop, far from the target.

"Okay, kids in the audience," Coach Blake continued. "That was Coach Preston's rendition of what not to do when trying to dunk a loser. Let's get serious and show everyone how it's done, Coach Preston. No more kidding around. We don't allow practice throws."

Coach Preston gripped the ball in both hands as if he were making a snowball. He took a few steps back and bumped into the gathering crowd. The pressure was mounting as he made his throw and missed for the second time.

"Saw-wing and a miss," Coach Blake rubbed it in. "Okay, Coach, now the pressure is on. Imagine this. It's the bottom of the tenth inning and everybody is tired. Your team is up by one run and wants to go home. Only problem is, bases are loaded with two outs and the count is full. If you throw a strike, you can go home a hero. But if you throw a ball, you walk in the tying run and become the goat. So what are you gonna be tonight Coach Preston, a hero or a goat?"

Whispers filled the swelling crowd as Coach Preston dragged his hand across his face in distress. I knew the pressure he was feeling for I faced it every time I took the mound. He gripped the ball tight and began his wind up as the crowd anticipated his throw. A loud thunk was heard when the ball hit the canvas and he cussed to himself under his breath.

Goat sounds and laughter soon erupted throughout the crowd as the humiliated Coach Preston pushed his way through the mob, followed by his wife and six-year-old son.

"You can run but you can't hide," Coach Blake yelled showing no sympathy. "At least on Mary's Dress Barn, we may have some little lambs, but we sure don't have any goats. So who's next? Three pitches for a dollar. Three strikes and you're out."

I wanted to keep watching but it was getting late. My eyes began to tear as I let out a long yawn, and I wove by people trying to get to a nearby exit. Coach Blake caught me off guard when he yelled, "Hey, look who's here. Isn't that Ace Sherman, the star pitcher?"

I pretended I didn't hear him and noticed everyone staring at me.

"Hey, Ace," Coach Blake insisted. "Rumor has it, you're the best pitcher in the ABYL. After your last performance, I'll bet you a dollar you couldn't hit the broad side of a barn, never mind this little red target."

"C'mon, Ace," a parent from the crowd yelled. "Someone has to dunk this loud mouth."

"Yeah, Ace," somebody else bellowed. "Dunk the bum."

"C'mon, Ace," Coach Blake refused to take no for an answer. "I'll put up the dollar. What do you have to lose? Three pitches for the fun of it. Let's see if you have what it takes to dunk me."

Reluctantly, I stood before Coach Blake with a ball in my hand. Silence had taken over the once rambunctious audience.

"I know you can do it," Coach Blake said all kidding aside. "Let's see the arm everyone knows you have."

I studied the target as I felt the weight of the ball. I took two steps back and then finally a third.

"C'mon, Ace," voices whispered throughout and then erupted with cheers as Coach Blake submerged out of sight into the barrel of cold water. "Way to go," I was encouraged as hands began slapping me on my back.

Coach Blake's head emerged from the depths of the tank sending out a stream of water from between his front teeth. A widening grin soon followed.

"Well, it's about time somebody dunked me," Coach Blake laughed as he made his way onto the perch. "But I think that was just a lucky throw. You'll never do it again."

"Dunk him again!" a young boy shouted. "He's stupid."

"Hey," Coach Blake defended. "I'm not stupid. A little wet maybe, but not stupid."

"You can't be very smart if you give Ace three chances for free," the boy returned.

"Good point," Coach Blake admitted. "But if he dunks me again, he'll be playing third base for the rest of the season. So Ace, if you want to continue to pitch on my team, you had better miss."

"Dunk him, dunk him," the crowd chanted, and I was eager to please them. Coach Blake went under for a second time, and I was surrounded with applause.

"I mean it, Ace," Coach Blake egged on the crowd as he struggled to get back onto the perch. "You dunk me one more time and you'll be starting in the outfield. I mean it."

"Dunk him! Dunk him!" the crowd chanted louder than before and then howled with excitement as I hit my mark for the third time. The presence of hands patting me on my back and rubbing my head was overwhelming as the crowd congratulated me for my feat. At the time, I was in my glory.

Coach Blake struggled to get back onto the perch. As the water drained from his saturated clothes, he looked me in the eyes and said, "Okay, I've met my match. If you want any more chances, it'll cost you a buck. It's good to see you back."

I knew what he meant by his last statement and turned to him and said, "Thanks, Coach, but I've got to get rested up for the next game. I'll see you at practice."

I left the church bazaar feeling good about myself, and since that night, the friendship between Coach Blake and I began to grow.

"So, you mean to tell me that it took a silly dunk tank to help you regain your confidence to continue pitching?" Skip Freeman interrupted.

"I think Coach Blake's heckling tactics had more to do with it than anything," Ace admitted. "I think the atmosphere of the crowd at the bazaar made it seem like a real baseball game situation. That night, Coach Blake kept things serious but fun like baseball was originally meant to be. I'll never forget him for that night, even though I don't think he planned on this happening. It just happened that way. It was quite bizarre, with no pun intended."

"Quite bizarre indeed," Skip said in closing. "And when we

return, we'll find out how Tim "The Ace" Sherman's ABYL season

continued. We'll be right back after a word from our sponsor."

The Franchise Player

"I'll bet that any of you that began watching SNN's exclusive interview with Tim "The Ace" Sherman haven't left your seats yet," Skip Freeman announced. "I myself can't wait to hear what's about to come next. Now to briefly recap where we left off; it would appear that Ace seemed to have regained his confidence with his pitching in a most unusual place one night at a church bazaar dunking tank. I'm sure his season really began to take off."

"It wasn't as simple as that," Coach Blake pointed out. "Ace still had to prove to me and him during an actual game that he still had control of his pitching arm. A church bazaar dunk tank and a real game are two completely different situations."

"He's right," Ace agreed. "I still hadn't pitched since the game I was switched to third base, and as a team, we needed to have another practice before our next game. Unfortunately, the practice that Coach Blake had scheduled for us was canceled due to him working late at the Newport Sneaker plant.

I was determined to practice with or without the team and tried to make arrangements with Eddie, my neighbor, but he was unable to help out. Having no other choice, I set out to the ballfield alone with a five-gallon bucket of balls and an old T-shirt. The T-shirt, which was used as a strike zone would be tied to the chain link fence backstop. This was the closest thing to a catcher that I had and gave me some kind of target to aim my pitching.

As I warmed up my arm, each time I hit the dangling T-shirt, I thought of my Dad. Normally, it would be him behind the plate as catcher but his job forced him to travel. He came up with the T-shirt idea knowing he wouldn't always be there for me when I needed to practice. I think he missed our time together because whenever he'd call home, he'd always ask how I did at a game or practice. I liked that about him and he's one of the reasons I tried so hard. Unlike many Dads, I knew he really cared.

By the time I refilled the bucket for the fourth time, I seemed to be back in form. My arm was starting to feel sore, so after one more bucket load, I had planned to return home. As I set myself to throw my next pitch, a car had entered the parking lot. It was Coach

Blake, and that evening we had a talk that brought us even closer to being good friends."

"I thought that was you," Coach Blake said, walking out on the field. "I just happened to see you while driving home from work. How come you're here by yourself?"

"Because I need the practice," I admitted. "There was nobody else around so I came here by myself. This isn't the first time I've practiced alone."

"But why on earth didn't you call one of the other players from the team to practice with you?" Coach Blake asked. "Believe it or not, there were a few kids that were disappointed that I had canceled practice. I'm sure somebody would have joined you."

"I don't think so, Coach," I frowned. "After the way I pitched the last game, I don't think anyone on the team likes me."

"That's nonsense," Coach Blake assured me. "It isn't a case of them disliking you, it's just that they don't know you yet."

"If you say so, Coach," I said unconvinced.

"You know something, Ace?" he encouraged. "I wish more kids on the team had the spirit you have. I mean, some of the players were happy when I called to cancel practice, but it didn't stop you. You came out here by yourself, and that's the making of a franchise player."

"A franchise player?" I asked unaware. "What's a franchise player?"

"A franchise player is a person whose skills and personality can take charge of a losing team and help turn it around into a winner. I'm surprised you've never heard of that term. Those are the guys that get paid millions of dollars with the hope they can motivate the other players into trying harder and in time, make them winners."

"But isn't that the coach's job?" I asked. "To teach and motivate."

"In a sense," he explained. "I believe a coach's job is to see who has the most talent for a certain position on the team, and hopefully mold that player into becoming better. It's not always the position that player may want to hold or like, but it might be the position that person would excel in after being placed there. In many cases, a player may think third base is the position he'd be best at playing. But if he can't stop a hard hit grounder, I'll try him somewhere else. That same player might find his niche in the outfield because they can do a better job judging a ball's depth of field after it is hit. If that player catches every ball that's hit to them, that player will feel better about themselves, knowing they just made a good play. That's part of what's involved in my job as coach. And believe me, it's not an easy job because I'm not always right."

"So how do you figure I'm a franchise player?" I wondered.

"Let me put it this way," he said scratching his chin. "When you're out on the practice field, and you've got some out of shape coach yelling at you to do things that he probably couldn't do, you as a player resent that fact?"

"Yeah, like Coach Newport," I admitted. "I don't think he could bend over to tie his own shoes, yet he screams and yells when you can't run ten laps around the field after a long day of practice."

"Exactly, but when you're competing with another player for

the position you want on the team, you find yourself noticing the mistakes that player makes which causes the coach to sometimes lose their temper. You learn from that player not to make the same mistakes, and hopefully you beat out that player for your desired position on the team. It's all part of competition - knowing what to do and when to do it."

"I never thought of it that way," I realized. "When I think about it, I've always took notice when Coach Newport was chewing somebody out and learned not to make the same mistakes for fear of having him scream in my face at point blank range. I always hated when he humiliated a player in front of the whole team. I never liked that about him."

"Well, some coaches have different methods of getting their point across, but to scream in someone's face isn't a tactic I prefer to use. I want my players to learn and have fun in doing it. Everyone makes mistakes, and the only way you'll learn is by correcting past mistakes. That's why we practice."

"You're a smart coach," I told him. "And I'm glad to be a part of your team."

"Well, right now, Ace, you have a chance to become my franchise player. I need a player who gives our team a little self-respect. Someone the other teammates can look up to for leadership and pattern their own training habits to either impress you or, better yet, to take the load of carrying the team to victory off your shoulders. That's what our team needs right now from you - to become its leader."

"But I don't think I'm that player your looking for, Coach," I admitted. "I think Joey is the one you should be talking to. Everyone on the team looks up to him."

"I'll admit, Joey does have what it takes to win, but sometimes it takes more than one person trying their heart out. It usually starts out with one player, then the next thing you know it's two and then three. Before you know it, it suddenly becomes contagious and just about everybody is trying to take control as captain of the team. It's exciting to watch it take place, but the team has to start with somebody. Right now Joey isn't enough. We need a few more players like you to take charge. For our team to become a winner, we'll need another franchise player. That franchise player is

Tim Sherman."

"Well, I'll try, Coach, but I can't promise you anything," I said unsure. "I mean, if my teammates don't like me, it'll be pretty hard to lead them."

"That's not the talk of a franchise player," Coach Blake insisted. "That's the talk of a loser. Something you're not. All I can do is ask you to try. Trying is the key word here. Giving up doesn't exist in our vocabulary anymore. Giving up is for losers. There's no loser here. Nothing but winners."

Coach Blake glanced at his wristwatch and said, "Well since I'm here, do you want to pitch to a glove instead of a T-shirt? I've got a few more minutes before I have to report to my wife."

"I don't know, Coach," I said a little leery. "It's starting to get dark and it'll be hard for you to see the ball. I wouldn't want to bean the coach without any equipment on."

"Yeah, maybe you're right," Coach Blake agreed. "I'm a little hungry anyway. I really should get going."

"Me too. My mom doesn't like it when I'm out after dark. I think I'm gonna head on home so I don't get in any trouble."

"Can you use a lift?" he offered. "I have to go by your house to get home."

"Sure, that'll be great. Thanks."

As I relaxed in the front seat, I played with the buttons that mechanically adjusted the backrest. I pushed the button forward and the seat slowly inched its way up to an uncomfortable position. I then eased the button back, and the backrest gradually lowered back to where I was almost lying down. I glanced at Coach Blake to see if he was becoming annoyed but he just smiled, knowing I was being a kid.

I made one final adjustment, and as my view of the ceiling changed to where I could see the oncoming traffic, I noticed a wallet size photo of a young boy held in place by a paper clip on the sun visor. The boy was dressed in a baseball uniform, and he wasn't anybody I've ever seen in town.

"Who's the kid in the picture?" I asked. "Is he one of your

former franchise players from another team?"

"Oh, he was a franchise player, all right," Coach Blake sighed. "That's a picture of my son, Terry."

"So, how come you don't coach for his team?" I asked. "Most fathers usually coach the team that their own kid plays on. Is he all grown up now?"

"No," Coach Blake frowned. "That picture was taken two years ago. Terry died from an incurable blood disease. I guess the Good Lord needed a talented ball player."

"Gee, I'm sorry, Coach," I said uneasy. "I'm sure he was a good player having you as a father."

"Oh, he was quick," Coach Blake bragged. "He held the team record for stolen bases. Speedy Gonzales was his team nickname. Good ole Speedy."

"I'll bet you miss him," I said noticing a tear roll down Coach Blake's cheek.

"You don't know how much," he sniffled, trying to hold back

his tears. "That's one of the reasons why my wife and I are so involved with the league. When we watch you guys play, somehow you bring Terry back to life for us. He was just like you kids. It's too bad baseball season has to end. We really miss being around you kids."

"Well, it shows in your coaching, Coach. I'm just realizing that I've never met a coach that cares about the players as much as you do," I told him. "So many coaches favor their own kid on the team and couldn't care less about the other players. All they want to do is win, which there's nothing wrong with that, but sometimes they get obsessed with winning and it takes the fun out of the game. Coach Newport is a good example of that. We were going on our fourth straight undefeated season, and when I think about it, I really wasn't having much fun."

"I try to make it fun, but for me, sometimes it isn't," Coach Blake admitted. "There are a lot of things going on in the league that aren't too much fun. I'm not talking about the players, I'm talking about the other coaches. It's a little complicated for you to understand right now, and maybe if you become a coach someday,

I'll explain it to you."

"I think I have an idea of what you're talking about," I confessed. "I overheard a little bit of your conversation with Mr. Rogers the night of the bazaar."

"Well, whatever you overheard, you just pretend you never heard it. Some things have a way of working themselves out. All you need to worry about is getting the ball over the plate and let me worry about everything else. That's the coach's job, not the players."

"Hey, Coach! Stop! " I shouted. "You just passed my house."

"I'm sorry," he said as he slowed to a stop. "I guess I wasn't paying attention."

"Thanks for the ride, Coach. I'll see you at tomorrow's game."

"You bet kid-o," he smiled. "Get plenty of rest and don't forget your stuff in the back seat. Think about what we talked about. We really need to turn this season around."

"I will, Coach," I assured him. "Tomorrow night, we're

going to win."

The next day at school, I couldn't stop myself from watching the clock. Its hands seemed to have weights attached, holding them back from going forward. I couldn't concentrate on any of my studies and was yelled at frequently by my teacher for not paying attention. When that final bell rang at three o'clock, I rushed out the door and ran nonstop, nearly a mile, all the way home.

I was panting and out of breath when I entered the kitchen to greet my Mom, but she wasn't there. It was just my luck. The one day I wanted to get to the field early, there was no one available to drive me.

A note on the kitchen table only caused me further grief. It read:

Tim,

> *Your father is coming home a day early to watch your game. I went to the airport to pick him up and we should be back by 4:30.*

> *Please wait for us to get home.*

Love,

Mom

I was panic struck. The last time she had to pick my Dad up at the airport, the plane was delayed for an hour. If she planned on being home at 4:30 and there was an hour delay, she wouldn't be home on time to get me to the field before the game started. All I thought about was how disappointed Coach Blake would be if we forfeited another game because I didn't show up on time. Then the rest of the team would really hate me if that happened.

I paced the kitchen floor as if I were Coach Blake in the dugout, wondering what to do. Again, I was staring at the clock, but this time I wanted to attach weights to the hands in order to slow the time. I would do anything to see my parents walk through the door.

I hurried up to my room and dressed into my uniform, not wanting to waste any time in case they arrived early. That was wishful thinking, them arriving early, and by 4:15, I was now pacing the kitchen floor with my cleats on.

By 4:30, I couldn't stand waiting any longer. I should've been in the car by now and on my way to the field, but I wasn't. If I left the house right now to walk, I would just make it to the field on time. It was 4:31 and it seemed like an hour had passed. I was running out of time and options.

I came up with the idea to call Coach Blake for a ride. I thought maybe he could come get me and I'd just leave a note for my Mom. That was the plan. I dialed Coach Blake's phone number and a busy signal made my stomach churn.

That's okay, I thought, that means he's home. I hung up the phone then glanced at the clock. It was 4:32. I sprang toward the living room and pulled back the curtain to see if my parents were home. The driveway was vacant. I returned to the kitchen, pressing the redial button on the phone and to my relief it began to ring.

"C'mon, c'mon, pick up the phone," I muttered, and by the fourth ring, someone had answered.

"Hello, this is the Blake residence," Mrs. Blake politely replied.

"Mrs. Blake. Thank God you're still home," I interrupted as she continued to speak. "This is Tim Sherman. I need a ride to the game. Do you think the coach can swing by and pick me up?"

"Please leave your name and phone number after the tone," the recorded message replied. "And we'll get back to you as soon as we can."

My jaw gaped open as the tone filled my ear cavity like earache medicine, causing me a different type of pain. My eyes filled with tears, and I hung up the phone in a slow, zombie-like fashion. I looked up at the clock and it was 4:39. My chances of making it to the game were slim to none. I admitted defeat and slid back a chair and laid my head down on the kitchen table. I couldn't believe that this was happening.

Moments later, I heard a short blast of a horn. My head sprung up off the table and I nearly knocked over the chair as I dashed to the front door. Outside, my parents were in the idling car, waving and smiling, not knowing my sense of urgency. I grabbed my mitt and bolted out of the house. My hand yanked at the car door lever but the door wouldn't budge.

"Unlock the door!" I shouted in a panic. "I'm gonna be late!"

"Calm down, we've got plenty of time," my father assured

me as his hand reached behind his back and blindly felt for the lock button.

"C'mon, c'mon," I mumbled to myself while his hand fumbled about, still unable to feel for the button. My hand lay in wait, and I listened for that unlocking sound as if I were poised and ready to run a fifty-yard dash. I heard the click and my hand reacted without hesitation, as if the clicking sound were the starting bell to a race. I swung the door open and dove across the seat shouting, "Please, Mom, hurry!"

"Don't you think it would be nice if you said hello to your father?" she said as she turned around to back up the car. "After all, he did go out of his way to get here just to see you play."

"Hi, Dad," I said rolling my eyes. "Now can we go? I'm late as it is."

"Hi, Tim," he turned to me with a half-smile. "It's good to see you too."

Traffic signals seemed to stay red longer than usual on the way to the field, and the instant it turned green, I'd be informing my mother of the fact.

"It's green, Ma, it's green. You can go," I said fidgeting in back.

"I can see," she snarled. "What do you want me to do, drive over the car in front of me? Don't be such a back seat driver. You sound more like your father every day. Don't worry. I'll get you there."

"But I want to get there today," I said covering up my mouth, realizing I spoke out of turn.

"Tim, that's enough," my Dad interrupted, and I could see the anger in my mother's eyes as she stared back at me through the rear view mirror.

"I'm sorry, Mom," I apologized and kept my mouth shut the rest of the ride. The minute I saw her place the shifter into park, I was out of the car and sprinting to the dugout. I had already missed the pre-game warm ups and Coach Blake was giving last minute advice before I interrupted him with my presence.

"Hey, look who decided to show up," Joey announced. "It's Beanie Baby."

"Yeah, we're glad you could make it," Luke joined in on the ranting. "I thought we were gonna forfeit again because of you. Did you ever think about buying a watch? You know that gadget that helps you tell time? Or do you even know how to tell time?"

"That's enough of that," Coach Blake stepped in before tempers began to escalate.

"Sorry I'm late," I apologized and began to explain. "My Mom had to pick up my Dad at the airport and his flight was delayed. It wasn't my fault."

"It doesn't matter," Coach Blake said relieved. "You're here now and that's all that counts."

"Hey, isn't that Coach Preston over there?" I pointed out. "I didn't know we were playing his team tonight. Do you think he's still mad at you after what happened at the bazaar dunk tank?"

"Mad?" Joey asked. "Why, what happened at the bazaar?"

"What happened at the bazaar isn't important right now," Coach Blake said, wanting to change the subject. "What's important right now is figuring out how to beat these guys."

"You guys should've been there," I interrupted. "Coach Blake and Coach Preston were arguing about tonight's game. Preston said that we stink and we're a bunch of no-talent bums and that his team was gonna kill us tonight."

"What does he know?" Luke sneered. "They haven't even played us yet this season."

"Yeah, who does he think he is?" Roger, the shortstop, yelled, feeling insulted.

"Coach Blake stood up for us, though," I began fabricating a story. "You should have been there. It was awesome. Coach Blake got right in his face and told him that we were gonna kick his team's butt. Right, Coach?"

"Is that what I said?" Coach Blake said grinning, going along with the tale. "I guess I did say that," he paused noticing the team begin to show some pride within themselves. "So you know what we gotta do, don't you? Let's put our gloves together and go kick some butt!"

After the team gave out a roaring yell, we dispersed to our positions on the playing field. Coach Blake surprised me when he said, "Ace, you're pitching the first three innings."

"But I always close the game," I said, waiting for an explanation.

"I want to try something different tonight," he pointed out. "Maybe if you can shut them down the first three innings, they'll lose their confidence at the plate. Hopefully, Mike will be able to close the game pitching to a bunch of frustrated batters."

"But, Coach," I disagreed. "Let me…"

"Go warm up," he interrupted. "I need that franchise player tonight. This is your chance to take that first step. Go show our team some leadership."

"Okay, Coach," I reluctantly agreed. "I'll do my best."

"That's all I ask," he said rubbing my head. "And thanks for getting the team psyched up. I wasn't sure what I was going to say to get them motivated. Your little story seems to be working. They look sharp out there. Now get out there and strike out some batters."

I stood on the mound, staring at the hard edged face of Joey with his catcher's mitt outstretched. My first pitch left behind a cloud of dust and a loud slap from his mitt, and he tossed the ball back, nodding with approval. He returned to his stance to await my next pitch, but this time, he held out his mitt well out of the strike zone. I felt he was testing my accuracy so I aimed for his mitt. The ball landed dead center in his mitt and the force of the ball jerked his hand back. He smiled as he stood to throw the ball back and we finished my warmup without me missing my mark.

"Batter up!" the umpire yelled and I prepared myself by taking a deep breath as my opponent stood at home plate.

I eyed the batter and the position of Joey's glove. When I began my wind up, before I could follow through with my pitch, a chill went up my spine. The image of Coach Newport materialized, and the ball bounced just short of home plate and deflected off Joey's chest pad.

"Ball one!" the umpire shouted, and Joey shook his head in disgust as he tossed me the ball.

I rubbed my eyes trying to regain focus when my attention was caught by a young boy behind the backstop, who was perched on top of a man's shoulders.

"C'mon, Ace!" the boy shouted. "I know you can do it."

I peered at the boy not knowing who he was, but his face seemed so familiar. I glanced back at Coach Newport and knew what he would do next. As I tried to concentrate on the batter, I could see Coach Newport begin his sign. He tugged on his left ear with his right hand, but before he could drag his finger across his throat, the young boy distracted him. The boy pointed at Coach Newport's tie, and when he looked down, the boy pinged him in the nose. I released the ball and the umpire called a strike.

The distracted Coach Newport sprang his head up, knowing I defied him and squinted his eye along with a sneer.

"That's the way to do it!" the boy yelled. "C'mon. Strike him out!"

143

Again I began my windup, and again Coach Newport tugged on his ear.

"Hey, Coach Newport!" I heard the boy yell. "Your shoe is untied."

Before Coach Newport could drag his finger across his throat, he looked down at his shoe, and that's when I made my throw for another strike.

"That's the way, Ace!" the boy shouted. "All you need is one more."

I stared at the batter, and then at the boy, and finally at Coach Newport. The angered Coach Newport yanked on his left ear but the young boy reached around him and tapped on his shoulder. Thinking someone was behind him; Coach Newport became distracted and turned his head and was unable to complete his sign. I struck the batter out, only infuriating Coach Newport, and he began to quiver in frustration. He faded away from behind the backstop and left behind the boy, still perched on the man's shoulders, covering his mouth as he snickered.

"I've got to go now," the boy said waving his hand. "Make my Dad proud," his voice faded along with his image.

It was then when I realized who the boy was. It was the boy in the picture attached to Coach Blake's sun visor. It was Coach Blake's son, Terry.

I believed he must have come down from heaven to help me, and in having this belief, I was going to make sure it wouldn't be a wasted trip. The following batters that I faced all struck out, and Coach Newport's image never plagued me from behind the backstop. I was finally back in form, and we entered the fourth inning with a scoreless tie.

The team's morale was at its peak, and although we weren't winning, we weren't losing by the usual ten run margin at this point in the game. Mike, the closing pitcher, seemed to be the only player who didn't share the same enthusiasm as the rest of us, and when he took the mound for the first time, I stopped to encourage him.

"You look a little nervous," I told him. "It's only natural."

"It is?" he said uneasy. "How come you never look

nervous?"

"Believe me," I admitted, "I get butterflies in my stomach every time I take the mound. People think it's easy being a pitcher, and you and I both know we're the ones that usually get the blame if we lose."

"You're telling me," Mike's voice trembled. "I don't even want to be out here. This is the closest game we've ever been in thanks to you, and if I blow this game, I'll never hear the end of it."

"Just put on your game face and don't let the other team know you're afraid," I told him. "This inning, don't worry about speed so much, work on your accuracy. Then maybe in the next inning, you can combine the two."

"But if I lob the ball over the plate, they'll cream the ball," Mike responded.

"Don't you remember what Coach Blake said?" I reminded. "Just remember you've got eight other players to back you up. If they hit the ball and one of the fielders makes an error, they can't blame you, right? Just try not to walk anybody and throw it in the strike zone. I'm sure our fielders would like to see some action after watching nine strikeouts. You'll do fine. Trust me on this one."

"Okay, Ace," he said, swallowing. "Thanks."

"I'll be in right field waiting for a few fly balls," I smiled. "Don't let me fall asleep out there. I'll see you back in the dugout. Good luck."

My pep talk with Mike seemed to be working. As Mike had predicted, the other team was clobbering the ball, but our fielders were responding to the cause by making spectacular plays. By the top of the sixth inning, the game was still scoreless, and our team had a no-hitter going. Coach Preston's team was now about to get up, and an exuberant Coach Blake tried to rally us to a win with a pep talk of his own.

"For a bunch of no-talent bums," he opened, "you guys are really showing Coach Preston how to put his foot in his mouth. And, Mike, I don't know what happened to you out there, but keep it up. We've got a chance to win this game, so let's get out there and show Coach Preston that we came here to play. Now get out there and look sharp."

I never saw so many serious looking twelve-year-old players take the field with such confidence. The game's momentum had turned in our favor, and our team could almost taste certain victory for the first time. I stood in a distant right field and could see Coach Blake pacing in the dugout as Mike was about to throw his first pitch to start the inning.

The batter swung and grazed the ball, sending it straight up for an infield pop fly. Luke on third, Ted from second, and Roger the shortstop all glared up in the sky with their gloves raised, converging under the ball. When they collided, they lost sight of the ball, and it bounced off of Luke's shoulder and fell to the ground. The runner who thought he would be out changed his pace from a trot to a sprint and was safe at first base.

"You guys gotta call it," Coach Blake yelled from the dugout as dissension amongst the infielders began to take place.

"What are you doing?" Luke yelled at Roger. "It was my ball. I called it!"

"Well next time, don't whisper," Roger defended. "I didn't hear you."

"Don't worry about it," I yelled from right field. "We'll get 'em next time. Now get ready for the pitch."

The team settled back into the ready position, and Mike threw his next pitch. The batter connected with a line drive right into Nick's glove on first base. The runner on first base, who was a few steps off the bag at the time, was quickly tagged out for a double play.

"Yeah!" Coach Blake screamed from the dugout. "Now that's how you play baseball."

"Nice catch, Nicky Baby!" I cheered. "C'mon, Mike. One more out and we get our last ups."

Mike waved his glove in the air to me and an ever-present smile spread across his face. The team had regained its confidence and eagerly awaited the chance to make the last out.

Mike's first pitch was a hard fast ball that just missed the outside corner of home plate. His second pitch was just as hard but erratic and sailed over the batter's head.

"2 and 0!" the umpire shouted, and it seemed that the excitement was too much for Mike to handle.

"Take your time, Mike," Coach Blake encouraged. "Just put it over the plate."

Mike took a deep breath before throwing the ball, and it bounced in the dirt just short of the plate. He had lost his edge, and I felt he was trying too hard. I had a feeling he really wanted to strike this batter out as a personal triumph. I knew if I were pitching, I'd be striving for the same goal.

On his next pitch, he seemed to abandon the thought of a strike out and returned to his old form by lobbing the ball over the plate. The bat made contact, and the ball disappeared like a rocket over the left field fence for a game-leading home run. Everyone had their heads bowed in defeat as the other team celebrated by emptying the dugout, greeting the batter at home plate. Mike stood alone, crying on the mound, and Coach Blake called for a time out to see if

Mike felt he could continue.

I don't know what was said in their discussion, but I knew that Coach Blake would convince him to finish the inning. He knew that if Mike gave up now, all the confidence he gained in this outing would be lost and extremely hard to regain. Mike finished the inning with a strike out and our demoralized team entered the dugout as if we had already lost the game.

"Let's go, let's go," Coach Blake clapped his hands trying to lift our spirits. "This game isn't over yet. We need hits. We need hits. C'mon, who's up? Betty, who's up?"

"Let's see," she read off the lineup sheet. "John, then Gary, then Ace."

"Okay, John," he said in a frenzy. "Don't try to be a hero. Just get on base. C'mon, get out there."

After John and Gary both struck out, it was now up to me to keep us alive. There is nothing worse than making the last out in the game, especially when we had a chance to win. I wasn't about to let that happen and stood at the plate with my bat raised and ready to hit

151

anything in the strike zone.

My first swing was at a ball low and away, and I tried to check my swing, but I followed through for a strike. I knew I shouldn't have swung at that pitch and so did Coach Blake.

"Wait for your pitch!" Coach Blake yelled. "Use your head out there."

I looked the pitcher in the eye, and he hurled another fast ball right over the plate for a called strike. I should have swung.

"Now you gotta protect," Coach Blake said with concern. "That's two strikes."

Nothing was going to get by me now. I was determined to get a hit or a foul tip in order to stay alive. The next pitch that came in, I hit it, boy did I hit it!

On my way to first base, the tiny crowd roared as the ball sailed over the center fielder's head and rolled to the fence. The fielder was still chasing after the ball when I was about to round second. Coach Blake, who was the third base coach, was giving me the signal to slow down. Moments after reaching third, the ball came bouncing into the catcher leaving me with a stand up triple.

"Nice one, Ace" Coach Blake grinned. "And now it's Joey's turn. He's had a hot stick lately." He turned his attention to Joey and yelled above the crowd noise, "C'mon Joey. All we need is a single to bring Ace in. Wait for your pitch."

Joey seemed to ignore Coach Blake's advice, and he stared through the pitcher like a seasoned veteran. I think after my hit, the pitcher became rattled and was having trouble finding the strike zone. The count was full and the last three pitches were high and away, and Joey, in his desire to drive me home, foul tipped them all instead of taking a walk on balls. It was a classic standoff between a clutch hitter and a seasoned pitcher.

The next pitch thrown was low and well below the knees. Even Joey wouldn't have swung at such a bad pitch. He tossed his bat thinking it was a walk when the umpire changed the outcome of the game.

"Strike three, you're out of there!" the umpire yelled,

causing Joey to spin around and face the umpire.

"What?" Joey shrieked. "You call that a strike! It almost bounced off the plate."

At that point, Coach Blake lost control of his temper and stormed to the plate to try and reverse the umpire's bad call.

"You're kidding me, right?" he yelled inches away from the umpire's face. "He'd have to be playing golf to swing at a pitch like that. Give me a break here."

"You heard the call and he's out," the umpire stood his ground. "The game is over." Coach Blake spun around and cried out to the second base umpire, "Hey you, ump, what did you see? A ball or a strike?"

The umpire shrugged his shoulder as if he didn't see the pitch.

"What kind of answer is this?" Coach Blake shouted at him, mimicking the umpire by spastically shrugging his shoulders. "Was it a ball or a strike?"

The angered umpire raised his thumb, saying nothing, gesturing that Joey was out. Coach Blake admitted defeat and waved his hands in disgust as he turned his back to the umpire. To make matters worse, Coach Preston made his way out on the field.

"Hey, Blake, you wanna know what I saw?" Coach Preston taunted him. "I saw three pitches for a dollar. Three strikes and you're out. The joke is on you this time, Mr. 0 and 10."

Coach Blake gave him a look you would only find in an old time gangster movie, and if it were anybody but Coach Blake, there would have been trouble. He did the right thing by ignoring his remark and returned to the dugout telling the team to go shake hands with the opposing players.

"What a heartbreaking loss," Skip Freeman broke into Ace's story. "But I'm sure that wasn't the first or the last time an umpire made a bad call. It's just one of the things that you have to deal with when you're playing baseball."

"Unfortunately, that's true, Skip," Coach Blake agreed. "But sometimes a bad call like that can break a team's confidence. At zero

155

and ten, we had no chance of making the playoffs, and now the kids felt that even the umpires were determined to make sure we'd never get a win. It was a tough loss to overcome."

"So let me ask you this," Skip wondered. "Is that the game that you and Ace felt was better than his no-hitter in game seven of the World Series? I hope it was because were almost out of time on this show."

"I'm sorry, Skip, but it wasn't," Coach Blake pointed out. "How much time do we have?"

"We've got about fifteen minutes. Let's take a break for a brief message from our sponsors, and we'll wrap up the show with the game that Tim "The Ace" Sherman thinks was greater than his no-hitter in game seven of the World Series. Don't pick up that remote control because we'll be right back."

A Game to Remember

"Hello and welcome back to SNN's exclusive interview with Tim "The Ace" Sherman. I'm Skip Freeman along with special guest, Coach Cecil Blake, and we're about to wrap up today's show," Skip introduced. "If you've been watching this interview since the beginning, I'm sure you can't wait to hear about the game that Ace Sherman finds so memorable."

Skip paused to turn away from the camera and addressed both his guests. "So who would like to begin?" Skip asked. "You, Ace, or Coach Blake?"

The two longtime friends glanced at each other with Ace giving a shrug of his shoulders. Coach Blake took the opportunity to begin.

"I'd like to start, if you don't mind," Coach Blake insisted. "There were a lot of pre-game politics prior to that game and I'm sure even Ace would find them enlightening."

"I'm sure Ace doesn't have any objections," Skip concluded.

"The floor is yours, Coach Blake. Please begin."

On the morning of our season ending night game, I was on my way to work and couldn't help notice a huge banner hung outside the gate of the Newport Sneaker plant. I slowed my car to a crawl and read the words: CONGRATULATIONS COACH NEWPORT ON ANOTHER PERFECT SEASON.

My jaw hung open as I came to a complete stop, knowing the Newport Sneaks hadn't won their last game because they had to play my team tonight. I felt the banner was inappropriate and disrespectful and it infuriated me to the extent that I lost my temper.

I stepped on the gas pedal, and the tires screeched as I sped into my parking space. I came to an abrupt halt and slammed the car door behind myself. I was so upset, I rudely shunned greetings from my fellow workers when passing them in the corridor. Once inside my office, I sat behind my desk and spun my chair around to gaze out the window. The threatening storm clouds in the horizon mirrored my mood perfectly.

A buzzing of the intercom startled me, and I spun my chair

around, pressing the speak button to respond, "Production control, Cecil Blake speaking."

"Mr. Blake," a woman's voice returned. "This is Kimberly, Mr. Newport's secretary. Mr. Newport would like to see you in his office."

"Did he happen to mention why he wanted to see me?" I asked.

"No, he didn't, but he did want to see you right now," she returned. "He was very specific about that."

"Okay, tell him I'm on my way."

Kimberly was sitting behind her desk when I entered the lobby, and above her was another banner. This banner, in my opinion, was far worse than the one hanging at the front gate. This one read: THE NEWPORT SNEAKS - THE NATIONAL ABYL WIN STREAK RECORD BREAKERS. I was outraged that everyone assumed that my team was going to lose.

"Hello, Kimberly," I said staring up. "Nice banner."

"Isn't it though?" she said glowing. "This is so exciting. I'll bet half of the town will be at the game tonight. I know I'll be there. Are you going?"

"I have no choice," I said with eyebrows raised. "I'm the coach of the other team."

Her exuberant smile vanished as her front teeth bit down on her lower lip. She quickly changed the subject by saying, "Excuse me, I'll go tell Mr. Newport that you're here."

"You do that," I coldly replied and she tapped on the door before entering Mr. Newport's office.

"He's ready for you," she said on her way back to her desk. "Go on in."

"Good morning, Cecil," Mr. Newport said smiling. "Close the door and have a seat. It's time you and I had a little chat."

Mr. Newport leaned back in his plush leather chair, and to his left and right were two tripod easels. They displayed graphs containing information on the sales figures of the various types of sneakers that his factory produced.

"I can't help but notice the impressive figures on the chart," I opened. "It would appear that sales are on the rise."

"Yes they are, Cecil," Mr. Newport returned. "I commend you on the job you've done in production control. It seems like ever since you became part of the Newport team, sales have increased by 20 percent. I'm very impressed."

"Thank you, Mr. Newport," I said more relaxed. "I'm just doing my job."

"But if you'll notice on the graph, only one of our products is in decline," he returned and pointed to the line that was dipping down. "The Newport cleats, our most expensive product to make, are clearly lagging in sales. That's what I wanted to talk to you about."

"I was aware of the decline in sales long ago and couldn't understand why. I decided to do an experiment with my own team and fitted them all with a pair of Newport cleats. By the third game, I noticed that they were all wearing their other cleats. When I asked them why they weren't wearing our product, they said that the arches of their feet hurt days after each time they wore them. I think you should be having a meeting with the design department and not me. If they could design a more comfortable sole, I guarantee sales will increase."

"That's one possibility," he agreed, "but an expensive possibility. To redesign our cleat would mean costly adjustments to our machinery and too much time spent on retraining our employees. Both you and I know that lost time is lost money."

"But if you took the time to redesign the cleat," I said in my defense. "Wouldn't the improvement lead to more sales and make up the difference of any lost time or money?"

"Again, I agree with you," he returned. "But I've researched the idea, and it would be years before I saw any profit. I did find a simple solution though."

"Really," I asked unaware. "And what have you discovered?"

"Did you ever hear the expression *the power of advertising?*" he asked peering forward.

"Yes, but that's not my department," I confessed.

"Well the power of advertising works," he explained. "A name means everything. You can have a mediocre product with a well-known name and people will buy it because of the name. Shoppers usually choose between two or three leading brands and will usually buy the name brand their most familiar with, from ads. If it's advertised on TV, it has to be good, right?"

"You're losing me here, Mr. Newport," I said confused. "What's this have to do with me? I'm not in the promotion department."

"That's where you're wrong, Cecil," he said leaning forward in his chair. "It has a lot to do with you, but you don't realize it yet. You see, one of the main problems with my company is that my name is only known locally, here in Pennsylvania. To advertise nationally without the proper gimmick would be a gamble. That's why tonight's game is so important. It's the gimmick my company needs to begin a national ad campaign."

"So what you're saying is that if your team breaks the ABYL

win streak record, the Newport cleat line will increase in sales without making any improvements to the shoe?"

"That's exactly what I'm saying," he boasted. "This record hasn't been broken in twenty years. Of course sales will increase. Let me show you one of the sample ads."

The excited Mr. Newport stood up from his seat and removed a graph from one of the easels. He revealed a blown up team photo of the Newport Sneaks with the caption: The Newport Sneaks: The best team in ABYL history. Thanks to Newport cleats.

"If this ad doesn't sell cleats, nothing will," Mr. Newport raved. "Just imagine all the kids that see this ad and what they'll think. I'll bet the first thing on their equipment list next season will be to buy a pair of Newport cleats. We won't be able to keep up with the demand. Don't you agree?"

"It just might work but your team picture is a little outdated," I pointed out. "Ace is on my team now."

"Oh, this is just a sample," he said. "Maybe I'll use a picture of the kids piling on the pitcher after the last out. Hey, that's an idea."

"I don't mean to be a party pooper," I interrupted his fantasy. "But, what if my team wins?"

His gleaming face turned blank and expressionless and his nostrils flared out when he said, "I don't think you understand what we've been talking about, Mr. Blake," his voice began to rise. "The Newport Sneaks will win. Do I make myself clear?"

"So, what you're asking me to do is to throw the game?" I asked in disbelief. "I don't have any control over how my kids will play. It's the last game of the season, and I'm sure they'll want to go out with a win. Especially against your team."

"Your team is zero and eleven. I doubt very much that your team is capable of winning, but I don't want to take any chances. I just want you to know where I stand on this issue. If there's any way you can guarantee me a win, you'll surely be rewarded."

"How could I possibly guarantee anything?" I pleaded. "These are kids we're talking about. Anything can happen in baseball."

"Let me help you out with this," he suggested. "Why don't you have Ace pitch the first three innings and my team will take it from there? That's all I'm asking."

"But my other pitcher isn't confident enough to close a game of this magnitude. He'll be a nervous wreck. I couldn't do that to any kid."

"Let me put it this way," Mr. Newport analogized. "Think of this company as your team and you're just a player. I'm the coach and I tell you to bunt. You want to be the hero, and instead of bunting, you try and hit the game winning home run and strike out in the process. That's not what I would call being a team player. As punishment, I have you sit the bench, and now you're unable to play. If you had listened to the coach, you would still be in the game like the rest of the team players and not on the bench. Now do you understand what I'm saying?"

"I think I understand, Mr. Newport," I said disappointed. "As long as I pitch Ace the first three innings, I stay on the team. But if I close the game with Ace, I sit the bench. A park bench to be more specific."

"Exactly, Mr. Blake. I couldn't have said it better myself," he grinned and reached out his arm to shake hands. "So you're going to be a team player, right?"

I said nothing in return and reluctantly shook his hand.

"Now wait just a minute here," Skip Freeman interrupted. "Do you mean to tell me that by shaking Mr. Newport's hand, you agreed to throw the game by pitching Ace first? That doesn't sound like you, Cecil."

"Let's not jump to conclusions here, Skip," Coach Blake defended. "I had no intention of selling out to Mr. Newport, even if it meant losing my job. After all, as a coach, I still hadn't won a game all season either. I wanted to win just as badly as the kids."

"I apologize for even thinking that," Skip admitted trying to hide his embarrassment. "Please continue."

I arrived at Newport Field just before game time and every available parking spot was taken. I dropped off the equipment bags, along with my wife, and had to park two blocks away. I was out of breath when I jogged into the dugout.

"Hey guys," I gasped. "Is everybody here?"

"Everybody except Ace," Joey responded. "Maybe he's afraid to play against his old team."

"He'll be here," I said with confidence. "I'm sure his parents are having the same problem I had when I arrived. No parking. This place is mobbed."

"I'll say," Luke added. "Even the TV news people are here. They were here before to interview you, but you weren't here yet. Now they're over talking to Coach Newport. See 'em?"

My attention drew to the fanfare surrounding Coach Newport. He stood like a politician, with his hands waving in the air as he made his speech. The attentive news lady held her microphone up near his mouth and the cameraman balanced the bulky camera on his shoulder as he zoomed in for a close up. I had to laugh when a gust of wind hurled a napkin across Coach Newport's mouth and stuck to it as if it were glued. Undaunted, he pulled the napkin away and continued speaking.

I turned back to the boys and felt a chill from the stormy

winds that made our dugout feel like a wind tunnel. All the players were fidgeting, trying to stay warm, and goose pimples were ever present on everyone's arms.

"What a lousy night to end the season," I stated. "I just hope the rain holds off long enough for us to finish the game. So, are you guys ready?"

"Ready for what?" Luke sneered. "For the beating of our lives? We're gonna get killed tonight."

"Well, if you all feel that way, you're right. We won't stand a chance," I scolded. "Where on earth is Ace?"

"Here I am," Ace said out of breath. "I can't believe the crowd tonight. It's like a zoo out there."

"Sit, Ace," I said firmly. "I have a few things to say before we get started."

"But shouldn't we be on the field warming up?" Ace asked. "The game starts in ten minutes."

"We've got time," I said glancing at my watch. "What I have

to say is more important. Now listen up." I began to pace across the quiet dugout hoping I'd say the right thing to encourage my disillusioned team.

"I know it's been a long, difficult season for you guys," I opened. "But the one thing I admire most about this team is your courage to show up for every game, especially this one. Tonight we face one of the best teams in the country, not just Pennsylvania, but the country. It takes a lot of guts to take the field tonight, and I hope that none of you feel that we're not good enough to challenge them."

I singled out Luke with a stare and said, "As a matter of fact, let's settle this right now. Is there anybody here that wants me to go over and tell Coach Newport that we want to forfeit, that we're not good enough to play his team? Because I will!" No one said a word and Luke had bowed his head.

"Well, that's good," I continued. "How about if I go over to that news crew and tell them they should be interviewing our team because we're about to carry out one of the biggest upsets in league history. Yeah, I think that's what I'll do."

"No, Coach, no!" Joey shouted. "It'll be bad luck. Let's just go out and play and get this game over with. If we win, I'll be the first in line to sign autographs."

"All right then," I said in closing. "Let's put our gloves together and use our heads out there tonight. It's time to rumble."

Each player ran out on the field to their assigned positions, except for Mike and Ace. Neither knew who was going to start at pitching.

"So I'm in right field, right, Coach?" Ace asked only assuming.

"Nope, you're on the mound," I told him. "Maybe we'll have the same success we had like when we played Coach Preston."

"Yeah, but when I started the following game, we got clobbered," Ace argued. "C'mon, let me close this one."

"Yeah, Coach," Mike pleaded. "I hate being the closing pitcher. I'll take the mound first."

"Do you guys have wax in your ears or something?" I yelled.

"Or do you guys want to coach and I'll take the mound and pitch? Now get out there, Ace, and start warming up your arm. I don't want to hear another word."

The wind whipped across the field with inconsistent gusts, and Ace had trouble adjusting his throws. Thunder in the distance caused the ground to rumble, and the outfielders gazed up in search of lightning. The sun soon disappeared from behind the threatening clouds, and the ballpark lights flickered on to illuminate the field.

"Play ball!" the umpire shouted, and the first batter stood ready for Ace's pitch. Ace fired a hard fast ball that left the batter looking at a called strike. The wide-eyed batter stepped out of the batter's box and glanced over at Coach Newport for a sign. Coach Newport placed both hands on his head, then down to his hips. He kicked his right leg three times and then nodded his head.

I turned to my wife after seeing Coach Newport's sign and said, "Did you see that Betty? What's Newport doing out there?"

"I don't know Cecil," she laughed, "but I think he's doing the Macarena."

Ace followed with a curve ball and the batter stuck out his bat to lay down a bunt. It was now strike two and Coach Newport began a different dance of signaling.

"All that work for a bunt signal," I muttered to my wife. "Ole Newport is gonna be tired after this game."

Ace retired the side, striking out all three batters. I could sense a swing in momentum in our favor as each player asked who was batting first when they entered the dugout. They all wanted a crack at the Newport Sneaks and eagerly waited to hear the batting order.

"Ace is up first, then Joey and Nick," Betty announced with the rest of the team bellowing in disappointment.

Ace grabbed his bat and took a few practice swings as his old teammate warmed up his arm.

"If it isn't Jack-Ace," the pitcher insulted. "I see you've made a big impact in how your team finishes a game. You'll be zero and twelve after tonight."

Ace answered back by cracking the first pitch over the center fielder's head for a stand up double. Normally, a hit like that would've had the crowd screaming, but only a small portion of the crowd wanted us to win. The crowd was so quiet that you could hear Coach Newport above everyone else.

"See what happens when you shoot off your mouth," Coach Newport shouted. "If he scores, you're on the bench. You got that?"

The pitcher nodded his head in fear and now faced Joey at bat. The second he released the ball, Ace was off and running in an attempt to steal third. The catcher bobbled the ball and was late with his throw. Ace slid safely into third base, and now we threatened to score. All we needed was a sacrifice fly by any of our next two batters and we would score the first run.

"Time out," Coach Newport said in a panic and waved his entire infield in for a meeting. Veins appeared to be popping out of his head as he spoke, and his finger poked at the chest of the young pitcher. Whatever his strategy was, it surely had an impact, because Ace never scored due to our next three batters striking out.

Ace was determined not to go down without a fight, and he frustrated the Newport Sneaks by striking out the next six batters. It was the bottom of the third inning, with no score, and it was our turn at bat. Mike, the closing pitcher, sat nervously on the bench, biting his fingernails and there was no telling what would happen when he had to pitch. We needed a plan and Ace had an idea.

"Hey, Coach," Ace whispered. "I think I know how we can help out Mike when he takes the mound."

"Oh really?" I said willing to hear anything that would help us win. "What's your idea?"

"Well, seeing how I played for the Sneaks, I know which kids can pull the ball to the opposite field. Maybe we can bait a field by leaving it open, the batter will swing at anything, just to try and hit the ball into the unmanned field."

"I don't follow you," I said, confused. "Excuse me, Ace. Luke, go coach third base for me. I'll be out there in a minute. Okay, Ace, explain your plan one more time. I don't get it."

Ace knew what he wanted to say but was having trouble

explaining. His voice began to rise as he tried to get his point across.

"Let me put it this way," he said. "If I'm up at bat and I see the left fielder daydreaming or out of position, I'm definitely going to try and hit the ball to left field. I would swing at the very first pitch in order to hit it there before the coach or player noticed what was going on. If we have Gary set up more toward center field, then the trap will be set. That's when you give Mike the intentional walk signal and hopefully the batter will swing at a pitch well out of the strike zone."

"It sounds like it'll work, but how will the rest of the team know when to shift over in the outfield?"

"When I see the player who can pull the ball into left, I'll hold both of my arms up in the air. You can make it obvious by yelling to Gary to move over closer to center field. Then you give Mike his signal. If the decoy is toward my field in right, I'll automatically move over toward center field."

"Okay, Ace, we'll give it a try," I said unsure. "But I have to go coach third base in case we get any base runners. Explain your plan to everyone involved. I'll see you at the end of the inning."

I left the dugout to relieve Luke of his coaching duties at third base. Joey, who was up at bat, singled and then Nick managed to get on base due to an error made by the shortstop. The game became intense when Ted followed with a walk. The bases were loaded and there were no outs. If our team didn't score now, we would be in trouble because their best pitcher would be on the mound for the last three innings. Coach Newport knew this and made a strategic move.

"Time out!" Coach Newport yelled. "Pitching change," he said waiving his discouraged pitcher off the mound.

Out came Coach Newport's new ace, who gave a dejected glance to the now sobbing pitcher as they passed each other. I felt sorry for the boy who left the mound because Coach Newport showed him no sympathy. He followed him into the corner of the dugout and scolded him without mercy. It was a degrading exhibition of sportsmanship on Coach Newport's behalf, and I almost wanted to leave my coaching spot to tell him how I felt.

"Play ball!" the umpire shouted and the pitcher did just that. He struck out the next three batters, leaving the game scoreless after three innings.

"Okay, guys," I said as they gathered in the dugout, "Let's show 'em some defense. Make sure you guys watch for any signals from me in the dugout. Pay close attention out there."

Mike nervously took to the mound and struggled with his warm up as the wind blew dust in his eyes and paper plate litter across the field. I stood outside the dugout, watching Mike's every move, and that's when I felt a cold drop of rain hit me in the face. Lightning flashed and thunder roared causing alarm in the crowd and the first batter stood at home plate leaning into the prevailing wind.

His first pitch showed no sign that it would cross the plate and caught everyone off guard when a wind gust steered it over the outside corner for a called strike. Mike, who wasn't surprised with the call, followed through with the very same pitch and achieved the same results, another called strike. This only infuriated the batter and Coach Newport.

"What are you, a mannequin?" Coach Newport yelled from the third base line. "Now you gotta protect the plate."

Mike gave a smile of confidence and hurled the ball, high and inside, and the batter struck out, swinging at an awful pitch. He slammed the end of the bat to the ground and made room for the next batter.

From the dugout, I could see Ace in right field with both arms raised. The next batter up would be baited for our trap.

"Gary," I shouted to him in left field. "Move over!" Gary took a few steps toward center field and stopped. "Gary!" I yelled waving my arms. "Keep going until I tell you to stop."

He hesitantly side stepped closer and closer to John in center field, and when he was just about ten feet away from him, I signaled him to stop.

Coach Newport looked as if he were doing an Irish jig on the third base line and signaled his batter to pull the ball to left field. I watched the batter readjust his feet and I knew they fell for our trap. I whistled to Mike out on the mound and gave him our sign. My two fingers walked across the palm of my hand and he nodded, knowing what to do next. With a wink to Joey, he relayed my signal, and Joey stretched out his mitt well out of the strike zone.

Mike lobbed the ball so far out of the strike zone that the batter nearly stepped on home plate just to come close to hitting it. The ball hit the bat and spun backward over Joey's head for a foul tip strike and crashed into the backstop.

Coach Newport became outraged and began to yell. "What are you swinging at? That wasn't even close!" He shouted and turned away from the batter and took off his hat, slapping it against his leg.

I took advantage of Coach Newport's outburst and signaled Mike to throw a strike. Then with a silent wave of my hand, I signaled to Gary in left field to get back into position. Coach Newport, who was still in a tantrum, never noticed our defensive changes and proceeded to do his Irish jig near third base.

The batter swung at Mike's next pitch, making solid contact with the ball and pulled the ball toward left field. Gary merely had to take one step back and the ball landed in his awaiting glove. From the dugout, I could see the white from Gary's teeth as he grinned when he hurled the ball back to the infield.

"Beautiful catch," I congratulated Gary. "One out to go!" I shouted making sure Coach Newport could hear me. His sneer of disapproval let me know he was aware of my taunting.

"Nice move, Cecil," a voice came from the dugout entrance. "So, you're really trying to win this one, aren't you?"

"Hey, if it isn't Bruce Rogers," I smiled, shaking his hand. "Of course I am. So, when did you get here?"

"I've been here since the beginning," he informed me. "I think you've got Ole Newport worried for a change. I think this is the only real competition he's faced in his entire win streak."

"Hey, we didn't come here to lie down. We came to play," I bragged. "If Newport wants that win streak record, he's gonna have to earn it tonight."

I turned my attention back to the game, and Mike was in the

middle of his wind up. Ace, who was once in right field, had moved over toward John in center field to set our trap for the next batter. The only trouble was, I was distracted by Mr. Rogers and wasn't paying attention. I never gave Mike the intentional walk signal.

"Ace! Get back," I screamed as Mike released the ball. I couldn't bear to watch and covered my eyes hoping the batter would miss the pitch. All I heard was the crack of the bat, followed by a huge roar from the crowd. When I peeled my hands away from my face, my team was running in toward the dugout. They had gotten the last out.

"What happened?" I said in awe. "Who made the last out?"

"You mean you didn't see that line drive back to the pitcher?" Mr. Rogers said with enthusiasm. "What a catch!"

Everyone entered the dugout, screaming and cheering, congratulating Mike on his miraculous catch. There was a chaotic celebration in our dugout.

"I just stuck out my glove to protect myself from getting hit," Mike laughed. "And the ball landed right in my glove! What a lucky catch."

"Okay, guys. Let's settle down," I said trying to retain order. "Let's keep our luck going with our bats. Betty, what's the lineup for this inning?"

"John, Gary, then Ace," she informed us. "C'mon boys, let's see some hits."

"Yeah, you heard her!" I yelled. "Let's try and knock the wind out of them this inning because by the looks of the sky, this may be our last at bat. C'mon John, don't waste any time warming up. Get out there. It's starting to rain."

The rain and lightning increased in between every pitch. The wet ball caused John and Gary to hit soft grounders and they were both thrown out at first without a chance of making it safely. Now with two outs, Ace was left to get a rally going. I could only hope that the wet ball wouldn't cause Ace to ground out like John and Gary.

"C mon, Ace!" I cheered as he stood at the plate ready to swing. "Hit it like you did in the first inning. Get something started."

Ace stared at the pitcher as if he were in a trance. The pitcher looked away momentarily for a sign from Coach Newport. Coach Newport tugged on his left ear with his right hand and then slowly dragged his finger across his throat. The ball was released and was heading right for Ace. Ace quickly spun around to get out of the way but the ball landed with a thud, catching him square in the back. Ace knelt on the ground arching his back in obvious pain. I rushed to his side and a bolt of lightning flashed in the background, causing the field lights to go black.

"Are you all right?" I asked, rubbing his back. "I think that pitcher did that on purpose." Then the lights flickered back on.

"Did you happen to notice Coach Newport giving the pitcher any sign?" Ace asked as we walked to first base.

"Yeah," I told him. "He tugged on his ear then did something else, and then you were hit by the pitch. Why? What does it mean?"

"Well, if he finished his sign by dragging his finger across his throat, it's not the pitcher's fault. He was just doing what he was told. That was Coach Newport's signal for a bean pitch. I know the sign well. That's the sign he gave me when I beaned Pete. I should have known it would be coming."

"Why that dirty . . . ," I wanted to swear but bit my tongue. "So he wants to play rough, does he? You just keep your eyes on me over at third and wait for me to give you the signal to steal. We'll make him sorry he put you on base."

"Don't worry about me, Coach," Ace insisted. "I'll be stealing second base the first chance I get."

The rain dripped from my cap's brim on my way to the third base line, and Joey stood at the plate waiting to knock Ace home.

"Joey!" I shouted with both fists clenched for a bunt signal and he nodded, letting me know he understood.

The pitcher glanced at Coach Newport, then at Joey, and then over at Ace, watching for the steal. Ace seemed preoccupied by arching and rubbing his back, letting the pitcher believe he wasn't a threat to steal second. The moment the ball had left the pitcher's hand, Ace was off and running. Joey pulled out of his bunt stance and the confused catcher bobbled the ball and made an off-balanced throw over the second baseman's head.

Ace never broke his stride and rounded second on his way to third. The outfielder slipped in the wet grass and struggled to make the throw from his knees back to the pitcher. Ace, who was now leading toward home, dove safely back to third base before the pitcher made his throw to the third baseman.

"Hang onto the ball!" Coach Newport screamed in a panic. "You don't throw it to third, stupid! What if he missed the ball? He'd be on his way home. And you in the outfield! You should be backing up any throw to third. Did you guys suddenly forget how to play baseball? Use your heads out there."

Coach Newport stormed back into his dugout and threw his cap against the inner wall. The cautious third baseman walked the ball over, keeping an eye on Ace so he wouldn't try and steal home before placing it into the pitcher's glove. When he returned to third, he was muttering to himself and shaking his head. He turned to Ace and said, "That was a heads-up-play, Ace. I'll bet you're glad you're not on ole Windbag's team anymore."

"No, I miss the team," Ace said smiling. "It's just Coach Newport I could do without. Playing for him wasn't any fun but I'm sure having fun now."

"I know what you mean," he sighed. "I can't wait till this game is over so I can think about something other than baseball."

"Time!" the umpire shouted interrupting the game. "Coachs," he said, waving for both Coach Newport and me to have a meeting at home plate.

The three of us huddled in a semicircle away from any players. Coach Newport was red in the face, still angry over the last play, and wouldn't even look me in the eyes. The rain dripped off our caps as we awaited the umpire's announcement.

"This is how it's gonna be," the umpire said firmly. "One more bolt of lightning and I'm getting these kids off the field. It's my job to make sure these kids don't get hurt. You can make up the rest of the game tomorrow if necessary. Any questions?"

"I don't have a problem with that," I agreed. "Safety first."

"Coach Newport?" The umpire asked needing an answer. "Any problem with a possible delay?"

"You're the boss," he said in a dismal tone. "Let's get things moving before we all catch pneumonia."

"Okay. Let's play ball," the umpire concluded.

"Time out, ump," I requested. "I'll make it quick."

"Time!" the umpire shouted and the crowd booed with disapproval.

"Joey, c'mere," I said in a whisper and Joey trotted over, attentive to what I had to say. "Now pay attention. This is what I want you to do. I want to try a squeeze play by having you bunt. Now, this is important. If you miss the next pitch, you'll have two strikes. Do not attempt to bunt if you have two strikes because if the ball rolls foul after two strikes, it's an automatic out. Do you understand? Do not bunt after two strikes. Just swing away."

"Okay Coach," he understood. "Swing away after two strikes."

Joey stood at the plate, swinging his bat like he wanted to hit the ball out of the park. It was a clever decoy that caused the infielders to step back. When the pitch came down, Joey was in his bunt stance and the infielders scrambled in. The slippery ball glanced off the wet bat, spinning backward into the catcher's mask and dropped to the ground for strike two.

"Okay, Joey," I yelled. "Don't let me down. You know what to do."

"Get back. Get back!" Coach Newport shouted. "He's not gonna bunt!"

Joey stood expressionless at the plate, and I had seen that look before on him. There was no telling what he would do next after Coach Newport's last outburst. I could only hope that he'd swing away.

The pitch was thrown and Joey switched to a bunt position.

"No," I cringed as he lay down a beautiful bunt that trickled down the third base line.

"Let it roll foul! Let it roll foul!" Coach Newport screamed as Ace leaped over the ball on his way home.

The pitcher stood poised but panicky over the ball, hoping the ball would roll foul before Ace could score.

"Pick it up! Pick it up!" a father yelled from the crowd and the pitcher clutched the ball and hurled it home.

Lightning flashed as the ball met up with the catcher's glove, and Ace collided with the catcher, knocking him into the mud. The lights went black and out of the darkness was the umpire's call, "He's out!"

When the lights flickered back on, Ace and the catcher lay slumped across home plate. The ball was on the ground.

"He's safe!" the umpire reversed his call and by then, Joey was making his way to third.

"He's going to third! He's going to third!" The pitcher shouted, and the stunned catcher picked up the ball and hurled it over to third.

"He's out!" The umpire screamed. "Everybody off the field!" He said in a panic.

The boys raced off the field, fearing the array of lightning bolts and entered their assigned dugouts. Coach Newport arrogantly approached the umpire to protest his call at home.

"What do you mean he was safe at home?" Coach Newport stood nose to nose with the umpire.

"The catcher dropped the ball," he stood by his call. "So he's safe."

"But you called him out," he pleaded. "You heard him, Blake. Didn't you?"

"To be honest, Mr. Newport, all I heard was thunder," I fibbed.

"Oh, never mind," Coach Newport conceded. "We'll just finish the game tomorrow."

"Well that depends," The umpire noted. "What inning is it anyway?"

"We just completed the fourth inning," I was eager to point out.

"Oh, in that case," the umpire declared. "The game is over."

"What!" Coach Newport shrieked. "It can't be over! You said we could resume tomorrow if necessary. We've still got two innings to play!"

"You know the rules as well as I do," the umpire reminded. "After four complete innings, it's considered a complete game if it's a rain out. That last out at third base completed the inning. The game is over."

"Well, I'm going to protest your decision," Coach Newport snipped back. "This game can't be over."

"You do what you have to, but as it stands now, home team wins. I'm getting out of here before I get hit by lightning. If you were smart, you'd do the same."

"So, ump," I asked wanting to be sure. "So, my team won?"

"As far as I'm concerned," he returned as he slid off his chest pad.

"All right!" I let out a yell. "We won! Hey, Mary's Dress Barn, we won!"

The team emptied out of the dugout, hooting and howling with joy. They surrounded me and jumped onto my back. My legs became weak from their weight and I collapsed into the mud. I was now on the bottom of a huge pig-pile, laughing. Betty, who had joined the melee, was covered in mud on the outskirts of the pile.

"So, there you have it, Skip," Coach Blake finished. "That was the game that Ace and I felt was better than the no-hitter he pitched in game seven of the World Series. I guess it was one of those games where you just had to be there."

"Well, I must admit," Skip smiled. "That truly sounded like it was an exciting game. But there's one thing that still bothers me."

"And what might that be, Skip?" Coach Blake returned.

"Well, remember when Coach Newport asked you to pitch Ace in the first three innings, you more or less suggested to our audience that you wouldn't? So why did you close the game with Mike, instead of Ace?"

"I remember something that Coach Newport said to me in an earlier conversation and thought it was good advice. He said, 'Preparation is the key to success.' With the help of Bruce Rogers, who informed me of the four inning rule, and I knew that by the looks of the approaching storm that we would never be able to complete the entire game. By starting Ace, I was guaranteed at least three good innings and Coach Newport would never suspect a thing. I'm sure he thought that I was going to be his so-called team player."

"But what if your game plan backfired?" Skip pointed out. "What if the rain held off long enough to complete the game or even worse, what if the umpire was one of Coach Newport's team players and decided to let him finish the last two innings the next day?"

"Because it was only a regular season game," Coach Blake told him. "If it were a playoff game, it would have been an entirely different set of rules. It was a meaningless game as far as position in the standings. We had no chance for a playoff berth and the Newport Sneaks had already clinched their division. When the game was rained out after four innings, the rule book says that it's a completed game. There's no protesting it. There's no appeal to the state commissioner. The game is over. I was just lucky that the rain had shortened the game."

"Well thanks for clearing that up for us, Coach. I guess by the sound of the theme music, we've overstayed our welcome and it's time to end the show."

The camera zoomed in for a close up of Skip and he gave his farewell, "Thank you for joining SNN's exclusive interview with Tim "The Ace" Sherman, along with his special guest, Coach Cecil Blake of the ABYL. So, you decide which game was more exciting. Was it Ace's no-hitter in game seven of the World Series or was it the game Mary's Dress Barn played against the streaking Newport Sneaks?

Thank you for joining us. I'm Skip Freeman and goodnight."

About the Author

L.P. Vine is a 57 year old, lifelong Connecticut resident. His passion has always been writing, but enjoys music, the outdoors, photography, and recently took up the art of wood carving.

He is currently dedicated to raising his ten year old granddaughter, who requires most of his spare time. She is his main priority but is making time to work on his next project.

CPSIA information can be obtained at www.ICGtesting.com
Printed in the USA
BVOW08s2137270616

453685BV00001B/32/P